THE TRANSLATION
OF FATHER TORTURO

Brendan Connell was born in Santa Fe, New Mexico, in 1970. His works of fiction include *Unpleasant Tales* (Eibonvale Press, 2013), *The Architect* (PS Publishing, 2012), *Lives of Notorious Cooks* (Chômu Press, 2012), *Miss Homicide Plays the Flute* (Eibonvale Press, 2013), *Jottings from a Far Away Place* (Snuggly Books, 2015), *Cannibals of West Papua* (Zagava, 2015), and *Pleasant Tales* (Eibonvale Press, 2017).

BRENDAN CONNELL

THE TRANSLATION
OF FATHER TORTURO

THIS IS A SNUGGLY BOOK

ISBN: 978-1-64525-029-6

To Frederick William Serafino Austin Lewis Mary Rolfe, Baron Corvo, for the design which I so meanly twisted.

CONTENTS

PREFACE

Written Nineteen Years After the Novel

*T*HE *Translation of Father Torturo* was written in the year 2001, over a period of three months, while I was residing in Besazio, Switzerland. It sat around for several years before being published, in 2005, by Prime Books, coincidentally one month after the death of Pope John Paul II.

In preparation for publication, I made some minor changes, principally updating the *lire* in the book to euros, to keep up with the changes in currency that had occurred in Italy. Unfortunately, however, the publisher not only refrained from editing the book themselves, but actually managed to introduce new errors into the text. The result, therefore, was far from satisfactory.

For the present text, I have made several hundred corrections and minor alterations, while refraining from changing the novel in any substantial way, in order to respect the book as it was originally written, faults and all.

THE TRANSLATION
OF FATHER TORTURO

Religion is a savage thing, like the universe it illuminates; savage, cold and bare, but infinitely strong.

—Robert Louis Stevenson

PREAMBLE

"HAL-LE-LU-JAH, hal-le-lu-u-jah-jah!"
Clouds of yellow smoke curled upward, like slowly revolving apparitions in the light of the immense and stately candles which were placed, dozen upon dozen, throughout the interior of the cathedral;—the ceiling, the cupola, seemingly as high over head as the night sky—thoroughly Romanesque, Byzantine, ornate décor protruding from all sides, dripping from above like stalactites, surging from the walls in carven stone and bronze panels, rising in grand pillars, winking in frescoed patches and chapels: the depiction of men at arms and others martyred; a few modern contrivances, the worst of contemporary art, dropped in, for juxtaposition, ugly slashes to enhance the already turbulent presence of the bizarre.

"Hal-le-lu-jah, hal-le-lu-u-u-jah-ah!"

The small figure stood before the seated gathering. She sang into the microphone in an untrained, slightly cacophonic voice that was yet buttered with faith. Sheathed in the coarse, clean costume of her calling, vestal white; eyes like raisins behind simple spectacles;

her voice uttered that modulated praise to Him, Master of all human affairs, Creator and Ruler of the universe.

The smoke plumed upward: aromatic, reminiscent of decomposed saints, hypnotic as it joined to the rhythmical chanting.

A beggar woman, a mad woman, obese and mal-formed (the majority of the weight being confined be-tween her lower torso and hams), struggled along one darkened side of the cathedral, the struggle all the more grim for the radical difference in length between her left leg and right. The disparity was made up by a pro-portionate wooden heel, which shuffled and clapped along the floor. Others, healthy in leg though feeble in mind, lay their hands on the sarcophagus of Saint Anthony.

But the vast majority of the visitors, pilgrims, rushed with remarkable haste onward, towards the brain of the cathedral. There a queue had formed and people pushed forward impatiently, rising on tip-toes and craning their necks. A child, a veritable cherub, innocent of social manners, wound its way ahead of the rest, its grandmother following in its wake, apologising as she went. It mounted the low steps on hands and knees and then, before the glass case, rose and stretched its arms out, the people parting on either side.

"Excuse me! Excuse me!" the grandmother said, hastening forward. And, with the words, "Oh, bam-bino," on her smiling lips, she hoisted the child up, so it could view what it had so impetuously sought after: a tongue mounted on a pin, like a dried cactus; a jaw, gums intact, teeth the colour of gorgonzola.

I

WHEN Father Torturo awoke it was 3 a.m.
He climbed out of the confessional, the base
of his black robe riding up, as did the leg of the pants
beneath, revealing an olive-coloured, hairy strip of
limb, the ankle dancing in a limp sock, the foot filling
out a well-polished shoe.

"Oof!" he said, cracking his back. "What an uncomfortable place to fall asleep in."

He rubbed his forehead, stretched himself and
blinked his eyes—two glassy balls, sangue de Cristo,
nearly as red as the glasses of merlot he had indulged
in earlier: a bottle between himself and Bishop Vivan,
and then a second to himself while alone in his room
reading over the *Dissertatio Epistologica de Ortu Animai
Humanae* of Gaultero Charleton.

A man in his mid to late-thirties, of good build,
with an aquiline nose and black, slightly thinning,
streaked-with-silver hair, Father Torturo was, at least
from appearances, the standard Italian Catholic priest.
His features were sombre and serious. Amongst his
brothers he was known for his thorough knowledge of

scripture and adamantine devotion to the calling; the lay-people admired him for his steady demeanour and the sound brevity of his advice.

"What should I do?" a woman once asked him. "I feel that I have nothing to live for."

"Nothing to live for?" he had replied, without flinching. "One would never guess it—judging by the size of your paunch."

By the scintillas which danced in her eyes and the foul rigour of her breath, it could be seen that, if the will to live had been threatening extinction within her, it was now revived to a healthy state of excitation. He noted that many good Christians liked a little rough treatment now and then, them gaining a certain morose satisfaction from being stroked with the fibres of sanctity. Often they needed to be whipped into the joy of life, prodded into the neighbourhood of the inviolable.

As a child he had been brutal, a kicker of cats, a resolute swatter of flies—one who delighted in passing gas against lighted candles. As a young man, under the auspices of the Church, he had grown hard, educated and inverted. He had studied the lives of the Saints, from those of universal fame down to others, who had as little renown as pismires. He savoured their histories, their sufferings, lapping them up as a poisoned man would draughts of emetic. He strove to lighten the darkness within him, and for every match he struck, a gust of cold, midnight wind responded, leaving him strolling sightless through bleak, empty space. As a man he was deliberate and blunt, a devotee of the Crucifixion.

The church was empty. He strode along its floors, his heels echoing through the vast chamber. His lips twitched slightly as he thought over the confessions of the evening. It was a thankless task, listening to people's disgusting trivialities. He glanced over toward the chapel of St. Felice, his gaze catching the tints of white flesh from Altichiero da Zevio's magnificent fresco: the ascetic limbs of a young man pinioned to the cross—a man scarcely younger than himself; his life-blood flowing easily from his crimson wounds. A well-formed horse's ass was nestled below, amongst indifferent onlookers. And now, because of this (those feeble drops of blood sprouting from effeminate palms), the porches of his, Xaverio Torturo's ears, were almost daily flooded with poison.

"*Latrina!*" he said aloud, his voice like a belch of geophysical steam.

Yes, he was more or less the toilet for the sins of others; the begrimed receptacle for their offences. Over the years, what filth had he not been made to bathe in, what garbage had he not been made swallow? The infidelity of women, the tomcatting of men, the gaunt perversions of the old, the raucous hellfire of the young. His heart was clouded, darker than the middle night and the shadows which lapped across his path, licking over his perambulating feet and rustling robe. He felt impure: the taste of old wine still clung to his tongue, the sound of sin still tingled his ears.

He fingered his rosary, turned to the right, crossed in front of the High Altar, stopped and looked: There was another Jesus; the Jesus Christ of Donatello, cast in black bronze, emaciated, suffering—dying the death of the righteous. The angels danced at his pierced feet, sung and played on harps and flutes. There were the panels depicting the miracles of Saint Anthony, which, as incredible in detail and craftsmanship as they were (profound in their beauty), inspired nothing in the priest but rancour, a feeling of ill will, as if his due rights, his fortune, had been unjustly snatched from him and cast to the paws of the lazy, sensual crowd: those hundreds of thousands who came each year, dined amply on baccalà alla padovana, and then, bellies distended with feed, came and set their gazes and greasy palms on the trophies—the bones that might have been his very own for all he had suffered, laboured in the cause of the Law and been spat upon with the trifling matters of cheesemongers' wives.

"What am I?" he snarled. "What am I anyhow? The younger brother, left disinherited. A miserable human creature; with this wretched flesh of mine. Thoroughly wretched! But you, Sir, hourly worshipped, mystically resurrected, have something better than that paltry flesh of yours."

Strange to say, the feeling that surged in him upon seeing this master work of art, this just representation of the Son of God, was not one of Humbleness, Faith or Love, but one of Jealousy—a green plant, prickly and monstrous that sprung from his bile.

"Damn me! Damn me," he muttered. "What kind of hypocrite am I," he thought, "to be running around, playing the faithful servant, all the while wishing to usurp the master." He grimaced. "You're an ungrateful goat," he told himself. "Throw yourself down before Him who has died for your transgressions—Throw yourself down, man! Throw yourself down and ask Him for His Forgiveness and Patience!"

He mounted the two steps, passed the microphone and pulpit, and walked across the red velvet rug. The mammoth cast candelabra of Andrea Riccio lined the way. The candles were extinguished, half-burnt and their wax looked especially pallid in the darkness, possessing the hue of dead flesh. The scene, frozen in bronze, bubbled before him: the symbology, the episode that, for a priest, was the focal point of life itself and the culmination of the religion he practised. True, worship was to be given to God alone, but it was awfully convenient to bow, salute with kisses and offer incense to these representations of the Lord and Saints. With the utmost difficulty Father Torturo roused in his breast a feeling of veneration, like a glow-worm endeavouring to find some rapid mode of exit, and, without allowing himself time to calculate the impossibility of the Presence, flung himself to the ground, where he beat his head upon the velvet rug. He crawled forward, clung to the base of the cross, caressed the cold metal and squeezed his eyes tight shut. He knew he should be crying. If he had any faith he should be crying.

"You hypocrite," he murmured, wriggling on the floor like a worm. "You stinking hypocrite. Do you really believe yourself to be any less——"

His self-disgust reached critical mass, burst, and mixed with the salts of his arrogance. He bucked, his body snapping up like the crack of a whip. His left temple smashed against the bronze toe of Jesus. He let out a white-hot scream and fell back to the floor. His ear was somewhat lacerated. His temple oozed blood. He clawed the carpet and felt the drool drip from his bottom lip.

"Hell and Damnation," he said and struggled to his feet, his frame trembling in agitation.

He felt the rosary still hanging in his fingers and clawed it into a ball. No one could say he had not tried, tried to love him. But in exchange, he had simply been kept down, like a servant or some lazy beggar. He ground the beads together in his grip, stepped back a few paces and turned. His soles slipped along the carpet and then clicked as they descended onto the hard floor.

II

"IT *is* a tragedy."

"It is a crisis which must be overcome."

"Have the police had any luck whatsoever in tracking down the vile culprits?"

"None. None whatsoever."

"And who do they suspect? There are rumours flying about, but they might easily have been created by the press. These journals, for the most part, are highly unscrupulous."

Cardinal Zuccarelli nodded his thin head in agreement. "Unfortunately," he said, "the speculations engaged in by the papers are as solid as our own. We have no more facts than they. As many valuables were left behind, I don't think it is a case of, as the Theodosian Code says, *nemo martyrem mercetur*, selling them, but more of some variety of sinister plot. If it was simply a matter of material gain I scarcely think that paintings by Tiepolo, Mantegna and Veronese would have been left behind."

"I personally would not be surprised if it was the work of the Jews," Bishop Vivan ejaculated with a sneer.

"It might as easily be Muslim radicals," the cardinal said, stroking the white mouse which sat perched in his pocket with one finger.

"Or the Buddhists."

"Indeed the Buddhists. Orientals will stop at nothing. They are quiet, but their very silence makes them all the more ominous."

"Well, at least the jaw was not taken," Vivan said presently.

"True, but the tongue is what people come to see. For some reason it is the tongue that fascinates, not the jaw."

The two men walked through the Prato della Valle, along one of the two straight paths that cut through the quadri-triangular landmark. Statues encircled the zone, adding an extreme measure of elegance to the scene, with their manneristic gestures and antique solemnity, that seemed to rub off on the holy pair as they strolled along, gracing the ground with their feet.

Cardinal Zuccarelli was the older of the two; a man fifty-four years of age, tall and thin, with an aquiline nose and penetrating eyes. His features were stiff and his flesh almost grey in tone. His bearing was serious and imposing. He had the elongated, severe look of a painting by El Greco. By his supreme gravity, it was obvious that he took himself and his office very seriously.

Vivan, the Bishop of Padua, was quite young for the position he held. He was forty-two. However, he looked even younger: his hair, which he wore just long enough to cover his ears, was full and black. His face was round and lively, the skin smooth and fresh as a boy's. Though he was not a fat man, he did have a delicate paunch which he stuck forward as he walked, or rather minced along. He had the elastic, red mouth of a sensualist and the sparkling eyes of a lively fellow.

The two men, as they walked side by side, gave a picture of two extremes in ecclesiastic behaviour.

A figure approached them from the far end of the path, tonsured head bent, the very muscles of the legs becoming obvious as they stretched out the fibre of his cassock in their advance, with steps long and brisk.

"It is Father Torturo," said Bishop Vivan.

"Yes, I have seen him before," said Cardinal Zuccarelli, peering forward with his keen black eyes. "I have seen him before, but I must say have had nothing to do with him. I suppose he is one of those inoffensive shadows which decorate the musty corners of our churches."

"Oh, he is as inoffensive as an insect—but he is far from being a fool. He is deliciously brilliant."

"Well, that is comforting. Inoffensive brilliance has a tendency to be far more useful than belligerent genius. Mousy men who know their grammar generally make good priests."

"Yes; he is an ideal priest."

"He appears to be hurt;—a bandaged head and hand. How extraordinary!"

"I believe he must have had an accident while doing gymnastics. A similar thing happened to him last year when he was showing the choirboys how to do some kind of special hand-stand he called 'the scorpion.'"

"So we have a priest who does gymnastics?"

"Yes," Bishop Vivan simpered, "the man is athletic to a remarkable degree. Though, in our line of work, callisthenics are not exactly orthodox, I cannot help but admire him, for a good physique is a beautiful thing."

Father Torturo by this time was quite near. The two ecclesiastics stopped, one tall, thin and somewhat grave, the other shorter, somewhat stouter, with a clear, effeminate, almost boyish face and a bow-like grace to his posture.

"How do you do father?" Cardinal Zuccarelli condescended to ask, as the other passed them, gaze still set on the ground, apparently unaware of their presence. Father Torturo looked up for an instant, nodded his head curtly, and then continued, moving away with his long, virile strides.

"The nerve!" Cardinal Zuccarelli gasped, his normally bloodless cheeks turning plum coloured. "The loathsome man hardly acknowledged my presence."

"I am afraid you will have to excuse him," the bishop said, touching the other's hand lightly. "I believe the poor fellow is overwrought over the loss of the tongue of the blessed St. Anthony. To my understanding, he has taken a temporary vow of silence."

"Has he taken a vow of pertness as well?"

"Oh, he is an odd fellow, I'll admit that," Vivan replied with a shrug of his shoulders. "But Your Holiness would be hard-pressed to find a more devoted servant."

"That may very well be," Zuccarelli said, slipping his arm through that of the younger man and resuming the stroll forward, "but we must remember that He most appreciates the humble servant. The proud servant often disdains those dirty little tasks which make up his daily duty. One day you find that he has been sweeping all the dust under the rug instead of doing things properly, and you say to yourself, 'Oh so that is why I have been sneezing so much!' Indeed, it is the humble servant He most appreciates." The mouse peeped out of his pocket and chirped. "Yes, Picolito," he said, stroking its little white head with his thumb. "Papa knows you're a teeny-tiny-humble servant."

The two men slowly moved through the Prato della Valle, and on towards Il Santo, the Cathedral of St. Anthony, their figures swaying slightly from side to side with each advancing step.

III

THE parents of Xaverio Torturo had been liquidated, due to a vendetta, when he was a boy of six. Found in the back bedroom of their palazzo, bodies chastised with more bullet holes than there are days in a week, and then severed into as many pieces as there are weeks in a year, they were the victims of a kind of crime which, to this day, is not uncommon in Italy. Undoubtedly he would have met the same fate, such revenges usually extending to the second and third generations, if he had not at the time been at his uncle Guido's house, playing at marbles with his cousin Marco, who was but a year younger than himself. When the news came that young Xaverio's house was wet with blood, he remained at his uncle's. Guido, according to the laws of vengeance, rooted out the murderers and did them one worse than was done to his own brother and sister-in-law. The uncle, adopting Xaverio into his household, became more like a father than an uncle; Marco more like a brother than a cousin.

"There is something funny about this boy," Guido's wife Bruna said to her husband one night. "I am afraid he will bring us trouble."

"Oh, I admit he is a bit naughty," Guido said with a shrug of his shoulders, "but that just proves that he has blood and not water in his veins. Frankly I am more worried about Marco; he is obedient at school, never complains and has yet to be caught stealing so much as an apple from the neighbour's tree."

"*Caro figliuolo*," Bruna sighed, thinking of her son.

Xaverio was certainly considered a wicked child. After class, he often beat the smaller boys mercilessly. The larger boys, those closer to his own size, he generally refrained from fighting. Instead, he simply humiliated them by time and again bettering them at sports and thrusting the knife of his tongue into their sides. No one dared cross him at school because it was known that his uncle was *un assassino*, and his nephew, therefore, if not demanding the utmost respect, was certainly not a boy to have as an enemy.

"You have to be careful," Bruna told him one day, upon catching him beating the neighbour's dog with a stick. "The witches like little boys like you. They like to eat little boys like you and send them to the devil."

Far from scaring Xaverio, however, this comment quite fascinated him. To be eaten by a witch and sent to the devil sounded, to his ears, like jolly fun.

Luckily for his teachers he was a brilliant child, and they could give him passing grades without in the least fudging it. It was true that he often made sarcastic remarks that made the class giggle and themselves look like fools, but the boy was marvellous in Italian grammar and, when asked a question concerning history or mathematics he was rarely wrong.

"He is intelligent," Bruna said, "but not half so sweet as Marco."

These words, though casually spoken, put a good deal of consternation into Guido's heart. He sincerely wished his son was not quite so sweet. He wanted him to be a bit rougher, a bit more like himself and less like his mother, whose qualities, though exemplary in womanhood, were not those he desired to see in a male,—particularly his own offspring.

"What did you do after school today?" he would ask.

"Played ball."

"With sides?"

"Yes. My side lost."

"Lost?"

"The other side cheated."

"But you didn't cheat?"

"No. Professor Lorenzo says that——"

"*Per la miseria!*" Guido interrupted, pinching the five fingers of his right hand together and waving them in front of his chin. "You need a real education. Get in a few fights. Fists are the best professors."

Meanwhile, he looked at his nephew, Xaverio, with a kind of awe. The boy was athletic, quick-witted, and as naughty as could very well be wished.

"Listen *figlio mio*," his uncle once told him, taking him on his lap. "It is obvious that, with your intelligence and spirit, a boy like you can grow up to be whatever he wants, either a criminal or a cardinal. In the history of our family we have many criminals, but not as yet a single cardinal. My confessor, Father

Falzon, has agreed to tutor you and see if you are fit for the calling. By the Madonna, I hope that you are. If you lead a religious life it might help to exonerate me from some of my sins."

Father Falzon, a crusty old priest with a reputation for misanthropy, somehow found the boy to his liking. Unlike other children, Xaverio did not talk much. He also brought his tutor stolen tobacco with every visit and this, for a man who often had to resort to smoking stale cigarette butts for lack of funds, was like a gift from heaven.

"Let me take a few puffs of this Saint Luis Rey," said the priest, his eyes emitting a dull lustre, "and then we will pray to the Christ, there above my bed, before having our lesson."

Father Falzon instilled in the child the habit of prayer, the habit of attempted communion with God. From his tattered breviary he began to teach Xaverio Latin, and was amazed with the rapid accomplishments of his student.

"I have never seen anyone pick up the Latin tongue so quickly," he told Guido. "A year ago he did not know the most basic elements of the language, and now he has already memorised the book of Genesis by heart."

What was even more amazing, was that, over the subsequent fourteen months, young Torturo memorised the entire rest of the Holy Bible, word for word, from Exodus all the way through Revelations. In less than two and a half years time, before he was yet a teenager, he had become as good of a Latin scholar as Father Falzon himself, who was certainly one of the few priests in the city who could genuinely understand the dead language.

In his own way, Xaverio became quite fond of the old priest.

Father Falzon, in his youth, had written a book of poetry titled *Un Cuore delle erbe*. The book had been much acclaimed, and had won several noteworthy prizes. It was his first and only published work, yet it was a minor classic.

Now, as chance would have it, Xaverio's school teacher, Professor Lorenzo, one day assigned the students to memorise one of the poems, *Amato Basilico*. Several boys gave vent to muffled laughter, and winked at each other.

"What is it you find so humorous Romeo?" the professor asked seriously.

"We know who wrote this," Romeo replied. "It's that old priest, Father Falzon. Me and Arnoldo——"

"Arnoldo and I," the professor corrected.

"Arnoldo and I passed by the church the other evening and saw him naked; we saw the old priest naked, drunk and sitting up in a pine tree."

That day, after school, Xaverio pummelled both boys vigorously, and advised them to watch their tongues.

Firmly established on the path of scholarship and entering his teenage years, when a keen and original intellect naturally finds itself drawn to the arcane, Xaverio proceeded to work his way through the old priest's entire library of texts, reading such books as the *Sermones Vulgares* and *Tractus de diversis materiss praedicabilibus* of Jacques de Vitry, the *Cisterciensis Dialogus*

Miraculroum of Caesar of Heisterbach and the *Exuviae Constantinopolitanae* of Count de Riant.

"Oh, that's a fine book," the old priest grimaced, coming upon Xaverio reading the *De fabulo equestris ordinis cosantiniani* of Marchese Scipione Maffei. "When you finish with that I will loan you his *Arte magica dileguata* and the *Arte magica annichilata*. These are hardly children's books and, unfortunately, many of my colleagues would say I am poisoning a young mind, but you are intelligent and will surely make your way through the classical writings without doing too much damage to your soul." (Here his top lip curled back, revealing a strip of pink, receding gums.) "To properly understand them though, I must say that a bit of knowledge of the Greek authors would do you good. I have a lovely Latin *Parua Naturia* of Aristotele Stagirita and——"

"I would prefer to read it in Greek," the boy said.

Father Falzon was dumbfounded. "Would you now?" he said scratching his head. "Well, my Greek is not as good as my Latin, but I could teach you some basic grammar and vocabulary I suppose."

"Please do. It is necessary for Bible study; and Uncle Guido will appreciate it."

"Yes," the father murmured, fingering the box of Montecristo No. 3's Xaverio had handed him that morning. "I am sure he will."

One day, upon visiting the father for his lesson, Xaverio found him sick in bed. His cheeks were pale and, in the weak light admitted through the aperture which some humorous architect called a window, appeared extraordinarily long. His nose was as red as coral. Black rings circled his eyes.

"I am afraid that I will not be able to give you lessons," the old man said.

"Maybe not today, but tomorrow."

"No, not today, tomorrow or the next day."

"What?"

"Bring me a glass of wine and water. The water is there, on the dresser. Look under my bed; you will find a bottle of Barbera. . . . Yes, that's it; a nice portion of wine—Please, not quite so much water!—There is no need to drown me."

When the boy had complied with his request, the old man held the glass of light red liquid to his lips and drained half its contents at a swallow. "Ah, that's better," he murmured, wiping his mouth with the back of his hand. "I had fire in my throat."

Xaverio looked at him seriously and asked: "So, you don't want to give me any more lessons?"

"It is not that," Father Falzon grinned hideously. "For one thing, I am not sure I have much left to teach you. You are a better latiniser than I, and, furthermore, your Greek is nearly at the same level."

"So you think I know enough; that is the reason?"

"No; I would still have you come around even if it was you who gave me lessons. To my feelings, Xaverio, you are my only ally here on earth. In the kingdom of heaven maybe I have a few friends; possibly even a connection or two downstairs; but here you are really my single interesting associate. This might surprise you, but many people look on me with suspicion. You ask why the lessons will end? I have spent my life in sedentary occupation; too much poring over books without the appropriate exercise; too much blood meat and maybe a sip too much wine. If you want a lesson then look at my sagging body, a mass of puss, fat, bile, blood and hair precariously clinging to a stack of weary bones. The only thing that keeps me attached to this bag of flesh is the thin stream of air which I laboriously drag in through my swollen lips and raw nostrils. The soul quivers, inconstant in the body like a bubble in water. Let me tell you frankly, without beating about the bush: I will be dead within the week."

"Dead?" the boy asked simply.

"Yes. I am ill. I had a dream last night that my body was consumed by maggots. After I die I want you to go to a seminary school."

"Fine."

"You have the intelligence to one day be a bishop, cardinal;—even Pope!"

"I will do as you wish."

"Go to my closet."

"Yes."

"You see the box?"

"This cardboard box?"

"Right."

"Should I open it?"

"No. Get it out of here. When I am dead, burn it."

"Burn it without opening it?"

"Yes; better you don't open it."

"Burn it?"

"Burn it."

"Fine."

"Do you want some advice?"

"Yes."

"Don't give yourself away. Not until you have them check-mated. You are smart, you stay relatively quiet. Better keep it that way . . . Look at me. I was never silent, never able to keep the words from falling from my mouth . . . I should have been a cardinal, not a damned putrid priest . . . Yes, stay quiet. That is the best gambit . . . Do you understand?"

"Yes."

"Now come closer . . . Kiss me; on the cheek . . . Do I smell so bad?"

"Yes; you do."

As Father Falzon predicted, he was dead four days later, of what malady the doctors were hesitant to report. Against the old priest's wishes, Xaverio opened the box. Inside were a number of books in Latin (The *Satyricon* of Petronius, *The Life of Heliogabalus* by Aelius Lampridius), an Italian copy of *Justine* by Donatien Alphonse François de Sade, as well as a vast assortment of improper contemporary literature. The boy scanned through the glossy illustrations of the journals, remarking on the depravity of the Italian presses, who certainly managed to outdo that of any other nation in the art of lascivious crudity and symbolic perverseness. The books in Latin and *Justine* he kept and read. The other literature, which was of no intellectual value to him, he distributed at the schoolyard after class. As he walked away he looked back, over his shoulder. He could see knots of boys stationed in front of the building, pushing each other and craning their necks over each other's shoulders while several, getting hold of some torn out page, scampered away gleefully, the obscene icons flashing in their clenched fists.

"You should have seen it, after school today," Marco told him that evening, when they were sitting in their room.

"You were there, after school?"

"Yes, helping Professor Lorenzo."

"And what happened?"

"We looked out the window and saw the boys—they all had bad magazines in their hands."

"And they were enjoying them?"

"They seemed to be. Professor Lorenzo ran out and caught two—Mario and Roberto. He asked them where they got the magazines from, but they would not answer. He beat their knuckles bloody with a ruler, but they still would not say."

"And the magazines?"

"Confiscated—in Professor Lorenzo's desk."

"Ahh."

"I wonder why."

"Why what?"

"Why the boys like those things."

Xaverio smiled contemptuously.

The next day he built a fire in the backyard and threw the empty box atop the flames.

"What are you doing?" his uncle asked, coming to the back door, a cigar clamped between his teeth.

"Fulfilling my teacher's last wishes," the boy responded gravely, his eyes fixed on the burning cardboard, black smoke curling up into the blue sky.

A week later he set off for the Collegio di SS Pietro e Paolo, located just outside the city of Parma.

"I wish I were going as well," Marco sighed, as they sat together, waiting for the train while Guido went off to buy the ticket.

"Your mother does too," Xaverio grinned.

"Yes, but it is father who makes the decisions, and I am afraid he has other things in mind for me besides praying."

"You'll manage," Xaverio said, taking the ticket from Guido as he walked up.

The train pulled in. Xaverio shook hands with Marco and kissed Guido on the cheek. Carrying his grip he boarded the iron beast which, squealing and moaning, carried him away, over rivers and past lakes, with snow-capped blue mountains behind them. He watched out the window, the farmers tilling the rich land, the land that had been marched over by armies, travelled by men of genius, fertilised by the bodies of hundreds of thousands, plague-stricken, and soaked with the blood of millions more—through war, treachery, the struggle for power and the unpluckable thorn in man called hate. He watched the businessmen who sat on the same train as him, sporting ostentatious gold watches and well-tailored suits that were worth a month's food. Then there were the women, the prima donnas, sheathed in costumes like snakes' skins which, by their movements, their motions and smiles, they seemed ever ambitious to shed. These were the people whose sins he must one day hear, the people that he must one day acquit, yet the people who, as sure as the moon did glow, he despised. He thought of his old friend, Father Falzon, who was more intelligent than any of these men of business, yet had lived his life without comfort and scarcely a pleasure outside of books, wine and tobacco. Lying dead he was, rotting in a poor man's grave.

"I'll be damned if I stay miserable for *them*," Xaverio murmured, looking at the garrulous crowd around him, which he thought more stupid than sheep, more dumb than oxen; the gregarious nature of the Italian people striking him at that moment, the first moment of his independence, as particularly distasteful.

IV

AT the Parma station, he was met by a young priest from the seminary, with a very high forehead showing the signs of early hair loss.

"Xaverio Torturo I presume?"

"Yes."

"Very well, come with me," the priest said, placing his hand on Xaverio's shoulder and guiding him out of the station. "You are a very handsome boy. Strong shoulders. You should do well."

Xaverio felt very much like breaking the fellow's fingers and telling him to go to hell, but he did not. He remembered the last words of Father Falzon and, lowering his gaze to the ground, kept silent. Pleased, the young priest smiled and patted him on the back.

Torturo's grip was put in the trunk of a two-seater. The priest unlocked the passenger's side, threw the keys in the air and, jauntily catching them in the other hand, stepped around to the driver's side. As they drove through the streets and then on to the edge of town where the seminary was, the priest never ceased talking, in his clipped, slightly arrogant voice, telling the boy about the town, its history and benefits, the seminary itself, the staff and the noteworthy students. On the whole, it was a well-practiced speech, one Xaverio was sure had been used on numerous others. He made a mental note to despise this young priest. The fellow's instant familiarity disgusted him to no small degree, and was a gross but prognostic taste of what life was to be away from home.

"Are you enjoying yourself?" the priest smiled, showing his teeth.

"Immensely," Xaverio replied.

He was determined to play his hand strategically.

At the seminary he was immediately introduced to the rector, an ash-coloured man with wide, pseudo-ecstatic eyes, who said to him:

"You have been born in lawful wedlock, have surpassed your twelfth year, and have indicated that you wish to be of service to the Church. You are here so that we may form Christ in you, for thereafter you are to form Christ in others."

Xaverio's nature was such that, whatever he did, fair or foul, he put his whole nature into it. The basic courses at the seminary were for him a simple matter. His spare time he devoted to his own studies and training in the gymnasium. He read like one possessed, lifted weights, boxed and practised handstands. At night, while the other boys slept, he devoted himself to rigorous meditation in the chapel. That there were things supramundane, things which were hidden from everyday eyes and mute to everyday ears, he knew through reading. It was not possible that there could be so many reports of the fantastic without them having any foundation in reality. The Holy Bible and the Lives of the Saints and desert fathers were full of the supernatural, not to mention all those numerous accounts he had come across in his other readings. Much of the material he had studied under Father Falzon's care certainly had a mystical flavour to it. He felt reasonably confident that the paranormal was an actual thing. It held great attraction for him; he was fascinated with the notion of miracles and aspired to gain a bit of mystical authority. All wicked temperaments like power, and it has been generally acknowledged that the greater part of the power of the universe is hidden. What was hidden, he desired to find, without in the least equating it with a straying from his religion. Some say that magic is but a disease, a corruption of religion, while others maintain that it is the natural preliminary phase of all religions. He found the former view to be hypocritical, inwardly professed the latter and, in the end, followed a creed all his own.

For the first two years he studied philosophy, elocution, geography, mathematics, natural sciences, and Church history. The last four years he studied Holy Scripture, rhetoric, English and French, apologetics, dogmatic, moral, and pastoral theology, liturgy, Gregorian chant, canon law and bookkeeping.

His means equated perfectly with his aims.

The fathers considered him very devout, though somewhat proud. He fasted often, kept four Lents a year, scrupulously fulfilled his duties and, when talking, did so to a purpose. He had been seen, on his knees before the image of Christ, for often five and six hours at a stretch, presumably in prayer. He would often walk in an orchard near the school, a work of the Greek or Latin fathers in one hand, and read aloud. He was humble before his betters, steady towards his equals and was not condescending towards those lower than himself. Though many were cautious with him and none loved him, his merits could not be denied. He had advocates rather than friends, but, more importantly, he had contracted no enemies.

He spent six years in ecclesiastical training, and was then ordained. By the age of twenty he had secured a doctorate in canon law. He was declared a fit ambassador of Christ. With his scholarship and obvious abilities, advancement seemed assured.

He was sent to the Archbishop of Ferrara, who was in need of a secretary. The archbishop was a fat, extremely oily looking man, with an immense liquidy second chin and a loose, sensual bottom lip. He offered his hand. Xaverio grasped it and felt the man's moist palm press against his own for a prolonged instant. The man regained his seat, and Xaverio sat opposite, on a low wooden chair. The bishop perused the letters of recommendation sent by the rector and other members of the seminary staff, occasionally raising his eyes and casting on Xaverio a thorough glance.

"Well," he said finally, setting down the papers, "you sound like an appealing young man: healthy; with good work capacity; you celebrate daily the Eucharist and the Liturgy of the Hours; no manifestations of hereditary illness in your family;—you should do just fine—as long as you studiously perform your duties."

Xaverio inclined his head and thanked the bishop.

"No need to mention it. You are consigned to my care as a son, and I have every intention of treating you as such."

Xaverio, now a relatively handsome and extraordinarily fit young man, went to sleep that night with his thoughts set on a grand career in the service of God. Though the way was surely difficult, it was at least possible. He was now in the service of the bishop. The bishop was obviously disposed in his favour. Advancement seemed, if not assured, surely probable. He closed his eyes and drifted to sleep. Around one in the morning he was awoken, his flesh being pressed against by a hot hirsute object and his bed suddenly cramped. He leaped up and began to defend himself, delivering rigorous blows with his fists in the dark and, when his arms grew tired of those, kicking with all his might until the thing flailed out of his bed and threw itself on the floor. The young man was disgusted and stirred by adrenaline. Not content with the small amount of ground gained, he took the water jug by his bedside and began to pummel the writhing mass with it. When the jug broke, he continued his work, utilising the broken handle and portion that remained intact in his hand, lashing out and letting it be known through his fury that he in no way approved of his sleep being disturbed in the aforementioned manner.

A number of the household's priests, undoubtedly hearing the scuffle, burst into the room. The light was turned on. The bishop lay on the floor, blood dripping from his nose and mouth. A half dozen rather serious

44

gashes marked his chest. Though Xaverio's conduct was certainly not approved of, no one dared call in the police. It would have been difficult to explain what the old ecclesiastic was doing in the young man's room, at that hour, stark naked, with a *consalateur* grasped in his hand.

The bishop was taken back to his room, to be attended to by the physician in ordinary. Torturo was shipped off post-haste to Padua with letters of introduction and a dossier worded in such a way as to let it be understood that the father was to be given the least possible room for advancement.

Distraught at his sudden change in fortunes, he internally cursed God, the priests and the boiling world. When duty did not call, he set off, like a blood-thirsty lion striding down the streets, to the edge of town, where for hours together he would prowl the hills, the wheels of his mind grinding to dust all the fantasies he had once entertained of an easy rise. His black image could be seen, disappearing amongst the trees, arms motioning impetuously and a fist occasionally flying heavenward where clenched it would tremble.

Gradually, however, after mature reflection, he became, not resigned to the situation, but able to accommodate himself to it. If this was the Church's way of saying "check," he would reorganise his forces until he could one day say, with a sardonic grin, "check mate."

At Padua, due to the influence of the Archbishop of Ferrara, his quick intelligence was altogether ignored and he was assigned the most ignoble of tasks. He was made to sweep and mop the floors of Il Santo, as well as clean the toilet stalls of the clergy residences. After supper he washed the dishes. In the early morning he polished the bronze sculptures and candelabra.

He performed these duties without complaint.

Gradually the incident in Ferrara was forgotten, all the more so as the archbishop of that diocese passed away in a manner which brought the Church but little glory. Torturo gradually burrowed his way into the realm of less filthy duties, toiling patiently and keeping his sights still keen on ultimate advancement.

He made marvellous use of what hours were left free to him. Twice a week he would take the train to Venice, which was a mere thirty minutes away, and visit a scholar, one Pierluigi De Vecchi, in the old Jewish section of town, who, for a small fee, taught him Hebrew and more than the basics of Talmudic lore and Kabbalistic philosophy. It was fitting he studied thus, in Venice, where the Talmuds were first collected into a concrete whole, and printed in the year 1520. Pierluigi was more than a mere academic; he was the bearer of an ancient and precious line of learning.

They read together the *Sepher Yetzirah* and the books of the Zohar. Pierluigi schooled him in the principles of Macroprosopus and Microprosopus, and also the doctrine of reincarnation. They read deeply into the works of Rabbi Judah Ha Lévi, Rabbi Moses Botarel, Ibn Gebirol of Cordova, and, in particular, *The Philosopher's Stone* of Rabbi Saadiah. He learned about the secret import of Tobias 6:18-19 concerning the roasting of a fish's heart in the bridal chamber, as well as all that was held in the extra-canonical passages of Schabbath, Adoba Zara and Sanhedrin.

Pierluigi particularly emphasised the power of sera-phim, cherubim, as well as instructing on the lore of Adam's other wife, Lilith, with whom he, the first man, had had alternative offspring.

"Oh, it is quite clear," Pierluigi said with glittering eyes, his lips pulling at an old tobacco pipe. "In Genesis five it says that Adam lived a hundred and thirty years, and begot a son to his own image and likeness. In the Hebrew this passage leaves no room for doubt;—if he begot a son in his own image and likeness, the explicit implication is that he had first begot a son *not in his own image and likeness*."

"Which is, I suppose, a confirmation that there are powers both good and evil."

"Oh, we are not talking about good and evil here. We are talking about the powers and things that be. The sons *in his own image* could hardly be called good; Cain shows us that by murdering his own brother. And those *not in his own image . . .*"

"Are not evil?"

"Well, no more so than suffering and death. When we slaughter the scapegoat, it cannot be considered an evil thing. By laying hands on it, it is imbued with the sins of the people, and thus we slaughter it;—its suffer-ing and death are not evil."

"But the laying on of hands;—is that a necessary facet of the ceremony?"

"Imposition of hands is vital to all the sacred per-formances. It is absolutely vital. Jacob bequeathed a blessing and inheritance to his two sons Ephraim and Manasses by placing his hands upon them. Aaron and his sons, the elders and the Levites lay their hands on the heads of the bullocks and rams prior to sacrificing them. Moses spread abroad his hands unto the Lord in order to make thunder and hail cease; and Joshua the son of Nun was full of the spirit of wisdom after Moses laid hands upon him."

"So the hands are the conveyors, the tools of some sort of . . . magic?"

"They are."

The library annexed to the University of Padua, which is one of the oldest universities in Europe, built by Sansovino in 1493, had an excellent collection of manuscripts, including even a few Assyrian tablets composed in cuneiform, copied from Babylonian originals, which dealt with the Chaldean period. These, with the help of an obliging professor, he managed to translate. They treated the subjects of astrology proper and medicinal magic as used by the Babylonian hierarchy, the Baru and Ashipu priests. Amongst the incantations there were the Shurpu, a spell for removing curses due to lawful contamination; Maklu, which was a counter-spell against wizards and witches; Utukki limmuti, which were a series of sixteen formulae against ghosts and demons; and Asaski marsuti, which were a series of twelve formulae against fevers and sickness.

"Naturally, a man like yourself must find these things somewhat scandalous," the professor said, as they gleaned over the script before them.

"Not in the least," Torturo replied. "I find it immensely interesting. It is, after all, part of the ancient history of our own Christian religion."

48

"Possibly, but many inveigh against such works as the teachings of the father of falsehoods."

"Often people warn us against things that they themselves do not understand. Christianity, after all, did most certainly evolve from animism, astrology, divination, magic and fetishism."

"That is not unlikely," the professor said with a smile. "But, you are taking evolution as your premise, which the Church is not yet reconciled to. Though you seem to be a logical man, the corporation you work for is not so broad-minded."

"I work for the corporation of *imga*; I work for the corporation of God, the corporation of the profound truth," Torturo replied with the utmost seriousness, looking gravely into the professor's eyes.

"Yes," the professor said, clearing his throat, adjusting his glasses and turning back to the manuscript that sat between the two men. "Well, in any case, let us get back to this section dealing with mysterious performances, *videlicet*: the recitation of formularies, gestures, and the blending of incongruous elements."

"Very well. The lines describing the transference of consciousness spell particularly interest me."

"Do they? I found some manuscript pages recently which, I believe, deal with the same subject."

"You believe?"

"Well, yes. I found the manuscript stuffed within the body of an old German Bible. There are a few phrases in Greek characters which point in the same direction as the lines to which you refer. The majority of the text is, however, in Hebrew, which, frankly, I know little of."

"It sounds very interesting."

"Yes; I will loan you the manuscript if you like."

"I would like nothing better."

The manuscript proved to be extremely interesting indeed. Written in a very small, concise hand, on fourteen strips of vellum and two of roan (the latter being in a rather deteriorated state), the material, though mostly in Hebrew characters, was not Hebrew, but a combination of Hebrew and transliterated Greek and Latin. No one without a fair knowledge of all three languages could have understood the contents. Torturo was fluent in two of the three languages and had come to understand the third tolerably well.

The title of the manuscript was *The Just Treatise of Transposition; Transferring the Substance of the Dead to the Living, and the Fundamental Nature of the Living to the Dead,* and claimed itself to be the work of Simeon ben Jochai. That it was written during, or just after the reign of the Emperor Titus seemed likely from certain passages;—though, judging from its style, it could have been composed anywhere from 50 to 300 A.D.

V

"*CIN-CIN.*"

The two men lifted the glasses to their lips and drank. The wine, though not especially good, was pleasant on the tongue. Outside it was wet and chilly. To be near a fire, drinking, whatever it might be, was a comfort. The light from the fire glowed on their faces: one had features soft and gentle, the other's were like stone. The men were nearly the same age, but one looked ten years older than the other.

"I will change my occupation," said the softer, younger-looking of the two.

"What?"

"Yes—it is only me and mother now. There is no longer any need to keep it up."

"But it is your livelihood!"

"I am amazed to hear you, to hear a man of your calling say such a thing!"

Torturo shrugged his shoulders. "I respect filial duty," he said.

"Even if it means slaying your neighbour?" Marco asked in a whisper. "I cannot believe you truly think that."

51

"They are only metaphorically your neighbours. You have been brought up to perform a certain task;—That is the blade of reality."

"But . . . But, living without morality: It sickens me!"

Torturo took a sip of his wine.

"A certain English psychologist once said that nature's order is far older and more established than our civilised human morality."

"Nature's order?"

"Certainly: by killing, you are following the dictates of nature."

Marco sighed. "You are smarter than me," he said, "but that does not make you right."

"No; it only makes me easy as to the ultimate fate of your soul."

Torturo lit a Parisienne and crumpled the empty pack in his palm.

"I wish I were a priest like you," Marco said.

Torturo smiled grimly. "And sometimes I wish I were a hired gun like you," he murmured.

The waiter, a young, spectacled man in his early twenties, approached the table.

"One . . . You can have one more," he said awkwardly. "We . . . You see, we close in thirty minutes. So, if . . . If you want another you can have it."

"Yes; one more glass, Baldo, and then we will go."

"Another red?"

"Yes."

"Yes, two more reds and a pack of Parisiennes."

Baldo walked off and soon returned with the wine and tobacco.

It was 2 a.m. when Baldo Sorrissi stepped out onto the via Guazzo, and closed and locked the door behind him. The restaurant, the Trattoria Potenza, a business he and his college mates had opened the year before, was going well and he had every reason to believe that the profits derived from polenta, spaghetti and baccalà would see him through to a *laurea*. He walked lightly along the cobbled street, mincing his steps with an air of importance.

It was a chilly January night. A nearly full moon swung overhead, occasionally obscured by sailing smudges of cloud. It had rained earlier in the evening and puddles had formed in the potholes along the narrow lane, which glinted with an oily light. Baldo lit a cigarette and turned up the collar of his jacket, in order to protect his sensitive neck from the cold. Grey smoke billowed from his nostrils and twisted from the cigarette end.

He turned right on the via Cappelli, past the closed shop fronts, with their spray-painted metal shutters drawn down, the soles of his shoes sounding crisp against the wet pavement. He flicked away his cigarette butt and stopped of a sudden to light another. As he stopped, he thought he heard the echo of footsteps behind him. He turned, but the street was black and empty. Adjusting his glasses, he smiled into the darkness, as if to show the person who was not there that he was at his ease, and then continued on his way, the perfume of a fresh cigarette pluming from his mouth. With moist, bud-like lips he gratified himself, inhaling deeply of the fragrant stream: the stalk of cheap tobacco which he imagined imbued him with a sort of offhand elegance. It was at times like these, when he was alone with no one about to provoke him into speaking, to hear the hesitating strains of his voice; it was times like these that he cherished: The night chill, black and romantic around him, his mind and mouth full of maleness, full of plans and possibilities, as the clouds sailed overhead, skirting before the moon.

He turned down the via Gorizia, a certain measure of jauntiness apparent in his aspiring step, as if the empty street, which he was walking down the middle of, was some kind of high profile catwalk with flashbulbs dazzling at every angle. The truth was, however ,that the street was dark, dirty and unglamorous in the extreme. Notorious it was, but for the historian, not the paparazzi. In 408 Alaric I had made it wet with Italian blood, letting the guts of man, woman and child feel the smoothness of Gothic cutlery. Shortly thereafter, in the year 452, the king of the Huns, Attila, dubbed the Scourge of God, more or less levelled the same street on his way to Rome. Indeed, it had always been a place for cruelty to deposit its gore, being a meeting place for the screams of the populace every time the tumultuous city of Padua changed hands, was conquered or reconquered. The fact that this was the battleground of kings did not in the least hamper Baldo's mincing gait.

He flicked away his cigarette butt and watched it arch up, trail through the air and expire in a damp gutter. He licked his lips. A whisper met his ears that made his breath stop.

He wheeled around.

"Baldo."

"Oh," Baldo said with some relief, "it's only you."

"Do you love me? You don't act like you love me any more."

"I do, *babbo*, but——"

The blade ran easily through the synthetic material of his jacket, pierced his belly and tickled the inside of his spine. It was rapidly withdrawn, and then continued its eager, blood spilling explorations, rising and falling again and again into the young man, pricking out his life. At first Baldo struggled feebly and let out a few low but horrific screams. Then, fallen to the wet pavement, he consigned himself to the rest of death and let the blade rape away his life . . . The rustle of a robe, the rapid, decided footsteps withdrew, leaving the body twisted in the centre of the street, the rain admixing its fluid with fierce history.

VI

AFTER doing fifty knee bends, twenty-five on each leg, hams lowered until they pressed firmly just above the heel, Father Torturo proceeded to do a set of one hundred push-ups, an amount he reiterated three times daily. His muscular body jack-knifed up and down on the floor, his chin and pectorals just barely gracing the ground before being thrust upward once more. An oily sweat added shine to his skin. An equal number of sit-ups followed, and he then poised himself in a shoulder stand for a quarter of an hour before advancing to a neck stand, a position he maintained unflinching for a full ten minutes. Arising, he bathed his hands and face in a basin of water, wiped his body with a moist towel, rubbed it down with Carapelli olive oil, and then proceeded to invest himself with cassock, his bearing maintaining an almost religious solemnity.

His room was furnished simply: a single, spring bed with a wooden cross nailed over it; a wooden table, which acted as desk; a small dresser whereon sat a rosary and an oval mirror the size of his hand; and a bookshelf, filled with a number of volumes, many of them with their spines torn off.

Father Torturo looked at himself in the mirror, combed his hair with a hard rubber comb and, taking up the rosary which sat on the dresser, left the room.

✳

Bishop Vivan sat at his desk, silently absorbed in a book. Every now and again he would reach down into the slightly open drawer and remove a brown chip of Kinder Surprise, letting it drift into the open pink of his mouth, to melt upon the soft surface of his tongue. A smile crossed his lips every time he read some particularly delightful passage in his literature, and an occasional agitated frown, when the drama became awful.

There was a knock at the large oaken door.

"Come in," the bishop said with a sigh, placing a floral-patterned bookmark between the leaves of his volume.

Father Torturo entered. His face was grave and his piercing eyes quickly scanned the room and took in the bishop opposite, a last piece of chocolate flitting between his lips.

"You requested my presence, Your Eminence," Torturo said thickly.

"Yes, I did," Vivan replied, laying down the book on the desk. "First of all, I would like to commend you on your vow of silence. Though it was only for a short while, it was a noble thing, and, in my opinion, marks you out among your fellows." He cleared his throat and licked his lips. "But, I must say that I was disappointed at your lack of courtesy the other day when Cardinal Zuccarelli and myself passed you on the Prato della Valle. He was a bit upset. I defended you of course.—But, in all truth, a slight lack of breeding was displayed on your part. I need not point out that being in the Cardinal's good graces can do you no harm, but could do you all the good in the world."

"I thank Your Eminence for your interest," Torturo said solemnly. And then, without in the least changing his expression: "You yourself are a perfect model of manners and, in the future, I would without doubt be wise to imitate you."

"Well then, enough said," the bishop replied with a magnificent flourish of his hand. "I don't like to be a prig you know;—but I figured a little advice was in order—But please, sit down. I have been dying for a sympathetic man to talk to. You look flushed, Torturo. Let me order us some tea. The refreshment will do you wonders."

The father seated himself on an uncushioned wooden chair, the most uncomfortable in the room, crossed one leg over the next and glared down, almost contemptuously at the bishop's small, effeminate form. Vivan looked up with his watery-blue, innocent boy's gaze.

"Your eyes are quite red," he said, in a hushed voice.

"You'll have to excuse me. I did not sleep much last night."

"Perusing some quaint, curious tome no doubt," the bishop giggled. He picked up the telephone, rang the outer office and ordered tea. "I myself," he continued. "I myself have been reading this marvellous little book." He lay his hand reverently on the cover. "There is a whole series, of literally hundreds of volumes, all dealing with these two delightful young men, Frank and Joe Hardy—brothers. They are honest, clean, god-fearing American boys of the sweetest water. The book we have before us, titled *Slip, Slide and Slapshot*, which, mind you, I am reading for the third time over, has a most fabulous plot. There is a girl named Jamie, a most atrocious little heretical wench, full of the folly of pride: Pride in being the star figure skater.—Naturally you can imagine this young woman, entrapped in the sin of narcissism and unjustly outraged at Joe because he accidentally chucks a shot right into her precious little ankle! So, imagine, she tries to get Joe excommunicated from the team! Thank God Frank and Chet—Chet is a magnificent young man (I imagine him an out-and-out blonde)—intercede. Then, inspired by the very Devil himself, Jamie accuses Joe of stealing her fuzzy white seal.—Oh, but I see I'm saying too much! Of course you want to read the book yourself and make your own discoveries. You will be enchanted. I will lend it to you when I am done. It might not be in Latin, but it none the less abounds in merit. Indeed," he concluded seriously, as if he was stating the most profound truth, "when it comes to simple God-honest purity of heart, we have much to learn from these Americans."

"Yes," Father Torturo said ironically, "they have many of the qualities of children."

Vivan smiled, obviously quite pleased with the conversation.

There was a soft tapping on the door.

"Ah, here is Gianni with the tea."

A young, handsome acolyte walked in carrying a tray on which sat tea for two and a plate of biscuits and crackers. Father Torturo scanned him from tip to toe: the rich black hair, corral lips, the slim, fit figure apparent even beneath ecclesiastic garments.

"You can set it down here, on my desk, Gianni," the bishop smiled.

"Yes, Your Eminence," the young man said quietly, slightly bowing, his eyes shining with an inward fire. He set the tray down gently, poured the tea and, with noiseless gait, departed.

"A beautiful, Catholic example of Christianity," the bishop sighed, dropping two lumps of sugar into his cup.

"A pleasant young man," Torturo murmured into his own unsweetened beverage.

"My dear priest," said Vivan presently, "do you like fine things?"

"Fine things? I do not approve of jewellery or ostentatious show of wealth if that is what you are referring to."

"No, silly! I mean food."

"Well, as you know, I enjoy a glass of good wine, or a slice of quality cheese as much as the next man. But I am not one to much indulge my appetite."

"Oh! Wine; cheese! Well—I have something for you anyhow!"

The bishop fished around in the drawer of his desk.

"Here, for the crackers," he said, producing a jar of caviar. "This one is quite splendid. I purchased it just this morning. Delicious Russian salmon roe!"

Thirty seconds later:

"And here: A pâté; a pâté de foie gras from France! With plenty of truffles I assure you."

"Bishop Vivan," Torturo said with mock-archness, "are you by any chance a gourmand?"

"Oh, Torturo! But you know I like fine things to taste!—Do you think we have enough crackers, or should I call Gianni for some more?"

There was a low knock on the door.

"What can it be now?" the bishop pouted. "Are my duties never done? Cannot I enjoy a peaceful cup of tea with one of my brethren? Come in," he called out, leaning back in his chair with the air of a Caesar.

An old woman of minute stature, crowned with a net of frosty white hair crept into the room. Her glazed eyes sought out Vivan.

"Mother!" he shouted, rising from his seat, cheeks flushed like coddling apples.

The woman muttered some words of apology for her intrusion, advanced to the bishop and, as he bent over and clasped her, planted a kiss on each glossy cheek.

"What a nice boy he is," she said, turning to Father Torturo, who had also risen and stood like a pillar several feet from the others, his cup still in his hand.

"The nicest," he said, with complete composure, softening his features with a staid and understanding smile.

The mother and son began to talk on subjects near and dear to themselves. Torturo swallowed his tea and, after giving a few well-turned compliments to Vivan's mother, took his leave.

"What a wonderful speaking voice your friend has," Signora Vivan remarked to her son when Torturo had left.

"Yes, I noticed it myself for the first time today. It is rather odd, I have known the man for a great while, but not until today did I realise what a luxurious voice he has. It is so handsome! I put it down to a blessing received from a vow a silence he recently took."

"He is a holy man," Signora Vivan said. "This morning, on my way to the market, I saw him preaching to the fishes."

"Oh, mother!" Vivan laughed, kissing her on the forehead. "You do get such outlandish ideas!"

"That may be—but I am certain it was him I saw standing on the bank of the Bachiglione River and preaching to the fishes. He must have been preaching on Matthew, because he said something about the land of Zabulon, and the land of Nephthalim. Your friend has quite a distinctive appearance, and as you yourself admitted, his speaking voice is something special;—He is a nice friend for you to have, Sebastianino—He is like a regular saint."

VII

THE man secured the button of his pants, looked down at the filthy receptacle, as unpleasant as any in Italy, ground level porcelain, muddied by the refuse of man, and ejected himself from the closet, onto the open courtyard. His hairline was much too low down on his forehead, and his countenance, if seen at close proximity, bore the unhealthy lustre of face paint. He walked across, through the door opposite and the kitchen area beyond, which was stacked high with sacks of flour and sugar. His half-finished cappuccino was still sitting on the table of the mirror-lined shop. He picked it up and drained it in a swallow, smacking his lips at the bitter-sweet flavour.

"How much?" he asked, approaching the counter.

"One euro, fifty."

He handed the shop attendant a five euro bill and received the change.

"*Grazie.*"

"*Grazie a lei.*"

He observed the chocolates ranged in the glass showcase below and, as he moved towards the exit, lingered at the freezer near the door, noting the sorbet stuffed lemons and oranges within, as well as the bright ice-cream, sculptured into red roses and small yellow ducklings.

"Anything else I can get for you?" the shop attendant called.

"No," the man answered and pushed open the door onto the street. He adjusted his tie, which strangled as if it had been a snake around his neck, took out a pack of Parisiennes and, lighting one, made his way along the via San Vittore to the via Carducci, which he crossed at a trot, avoiding a scooter which bore down on him with aggressive insistence. With long, virile strides he passed between the twin towers of the Museum of Torture, the perfume of tobacco wafting around him, and proceeded into the courtyard, the walls of which were embedded with plaques and bits of sculptured marble dating back to Roman decadence. Flicking away the half-consumed cigarette, he hastened into the left-hand door of the Church of St. Ambrose.

Half darkness; the indistinct smell of religion; cool as a tomb. He chuckled to himself and listened to his own footsteps click along the tiled floor of the church.

The city of Milan was in a state of emergency. Rome quaked. Italy roared. The entire Catholic world seethed with indignation. Television reporters formed an airtight barricade around the points of outrage. Helicopters swept through the sky, growling and marring it with their black profiles. The president of the United States said he was "shocked at the inappropriate behaviour" of the criminals and mispronounced the names of three saints, two countries and his own Chief-of-Staff. The Pope put all his energy into a five-minute speech, twelve words of which were articulated clearly enough to be paraphrased by every news agency from New Delhi to New York. The disappearance of St. Anthony's tongue had been generally regarded as a horrific prank, a grim occurrence, the equal of which would not likely happen again in any Christian's lifetime. This newest event, the ransacking of both the Basilica of Sant'Eustorgio and Church of St. Ambrose was regarded in all quarters in the light of a conspiracy. Detectives were imported from both France and England and given carte blanche status. Meanwhile, the Italian police force enacted measures in and around the city of Milan not seen since the days of Mussolini. At the border town of Ponte Chiasso searches were made, though primarily of male youths of non-European origin. A few sachets of marijuana were discovered, as well as a stash of zoophiliac photos, but nothing more.

In the city itself, detectives mulled over the evidence, which was actually quite sparse:

The tomb of St. Ambrose had been broken into, the bars severed by means of a simple hack-saw. The forearms of the saint had been forcefully removed. The two saints which lay on either side of Ambrose, St. Gervaso and St. Protaso, had each had their carpals abducted. The precious regalia of the three had been taken and their robes left in disarray, but undamaged. The nearby tomb of s.s. m.m. Naboree and Felice had been pried open, the weighty marble lid let crash to the ground. The ancient remnants of each lay strewn about, fibulas and tibias distinctly missing. The glass tomb of St. Savina was broken, femurs gone, skull pushed to one side and gold mask cast to the ground, slightly dinged. The tombs of St. Satio and St. Marcellina, the brother and sister of St. Ambrose, had been violated in turn, portions of each corpse missing, most items of obvious pecuniary value left behind, aside from the ring which had adorned St. Satio's finger.

The only piece of evidence introduced upon the scene by the culprits (for it was assumed to have been the work of a band) was a single cigarette butt, extinguished in front of Bernardino Luini's painting of the Madonna and Saint Gerolamo.

The scene at the Basilica of Sant'Eustorgio was similar. The main altar had been raided, the pieces stored therein, those of the saints Eustorgio, Magno and Onorato filched. The bars of the Sarcophagus of the Magi had been sawn away, the venerable remnants of the three wise men sadly abducted. In the Capella Portinari the top of the marble arc constructed by Giovanni di Balducci had been pried open and let fall to the ground, where it had cracked in half, the magnificent sculpting badly damaged. A portion of the legs of San Pietro had been removed. Additionally, the monument of sacred relics just outside the tomb had been ransacked, a number of treasured bones taken.

❋

He had caught the 5:25 train that morning from Milan Central Station bound for Venice, his costume consisting of jogging pants, a blue jumper and a New York Yankees baseball cap. His black hair was now a silvery blond and, aside from his eyes, which had an impenetrable and cold depth, he looked quite jaunty. The only other person in the carriage was a youngish American woman, her hand continually straying to her long, straight blonde hair to adjust it or thrust it back away from her eyes, and whose ample derriere easily filled the limitations of her seat. She smiled and flashed her slightly orgasmic eyes at the disguised Torturo. He nodded his head and remained impassive.

The train churned off into the wet, dark morning, the buildings and street lamps looking particularly haunting at that hour, the former but vaguely illumining empty streets, and the latter shuttered up, in the ugly, inhospitable way Italian establishments are at night. The young woman crossed one leg over the next and closed her eyes. Torturo gazed out the window at the flying blackness. Forty minutes later the train squeaked into Brescia, before continuing on, towards Verona. Passengers, many who had boarded the train the evening before, in places as far away as Germany and Belgium, began to emerge from the sleeping cars, yawning and scratching their backs and heads. The snack cart began to make its way along the side aisle, serving biscuits and what the attendant naïvely referred to (though with a certain degree of pride), as "German coffee."

"Café?" the attendant asked, poking his head in.

The young woman yawned and stretched her arms. "Yes—*Si, si,*" she said.

She paid the man, took out a book from her purse and, while sipping her coffee, read.

At Verona, Torturo stepped off the train, made his way to the news kiosk in three strides, bought the morning edition of the *Corriere della Sera*, and was back on the train in less than two minutes. He ran his tongue over his teeth as he read the headlines and, continuing on into the leading article, noted what a poor range of vocabulary the writer, one Giuseppe Brilli, had. The word "*scioccante*" was used five times in the space of two paragraphs, and the phrase "*criminali depravati*" over a dozen in the entire article.

"Literacy is certainly the death of literature," Torturo thought as he looked up and noticed the book the young woman was reading: King and Straub's *Black House.*

As the train pulled into Padua, which is less than an hour's ride beyond Verona, he peered up from his paper and out the window of the second class carriage. The sky was grey and softly lit, depositing drizzle which slid down the window like tears. Several passengers boarded the train, but none sat in the four empty seats of his carriage.

"We've been so lucky to have this compartment to ourselves," the woman across from him said in English. "I just hate it when it's full."

He gave an indulgent smile over the edge of his paper and shrugged his shoulders, signifying that he did not understand a word she said, though he understood her perfectly.

"Oh, I'm sorry," she smiled. "You don't understand English. I thought you did—The baseball cap you know."

"*Si, si!*" and then turning back to the journal, which was quite obviously written in Italian: "*Permesso.*"

Though his ticket would take him all the way to Venice, he got off at Mestre, the previous stop. With long, almost imperial strides he made his way to the opposite track and boarded the train for Trieste, which pulled out just seconds after the door shut behind him. He sat alone in a first-class carriage (ticket purchased three days previous at the Verona station), his luggage, which consisted of two Samsonite suitcases, stowed neatly overhead. The trip was uneventful. He looked out the window at the cows grazing in the wet, lush meadows. The farmers moved around their fields and barns, wearing broad-brimmed hats to keep the rain off their faces. After Monfalcone, the train ran along the Gulf of Trieste and Torturo looked out at the calm, though somewhat dismal Adriatic Sea, the waters appearing almost black in the morning light. Sloping down from his left were the hills of Slovenia. Behind him was the mass of Italy. He looked at his watch. It was 9:30. A quarter of an hour later the train pulled into the Trieste station. He deboarded, headed straight for the restrooms, which were completely empty, abandoned his wig and changed his clothes. The cap, jogging pants and jumper were stuffed in the trash receptacle, the sacerdotal robes resumed.

Despite the drizzle, which still persisted outside, he made his way on foot, a suitcase in each hand, to the local stop, some four blocks away. As luck would have it, he only had to wait for some five minutes before the small red trolley arrived, though he was fairly soaked through by the time he boarded. The three or four people who were on the transport nodded to him respectfully, their reverence being inspired not so much by his moist appearance as by the garments he wore. He sat down in one of the antique wooden seats, towards the front, where the sign still read, "Reserved for Veterans of the War," an indication of the age of the little trolley, which jolted into motion and wound through the empty streets of Trieste, past the rain dimpled harbour, which contained mammoth cargo ships, with dirty white characters inscribed on their sides, mostly in Russian and other Eastern European languages. The trolley reached the edge of town and gained grade, climbing up the steep hills towards the frontier, down below the harbour a gorgeous blue-grey against the gouged out blocks of buildings and the rich green, mist-wreathed hills. At the gorge it stopped, and funicular lines were attached. It continued airborne for a short distance and then resumed its route on tracks, to Villa Opicina, which was the end of the line.

Getting off the train, the conductor, a small, balding man, helped him with one of the suitcases, obviously considering it an act of devotion.

"Quite light," he commented, setting it down in the station bar.

"Yes," the father replied with a half smile. "I left my Bibles at home."

He then went to the phone booth, made a brief call, and returned to the station bar to have an espresso. He chatted casually with the fat woman behind the counter, complimented her on her Italian (she was Slovenian), had a second espresso and stepped outside. He smoked two cigarettes, paced back and forth for a quarter of an hour and then, just as he was lighting a third, Dr. Jure Štrekel pulled up, in a small white car with Slovenian plates.

The doctor, a man even larger than Father Torturo, with an extraordinarily thick frame and a huge black moustache spiking out of his pale, fat face, stepped out of the car, cracked his knuckles, opened the trunk and flung the two suitcases inside, a jaunty greeting flying off his lips.

"So, glad to have you back," he grinned as they drove away, his Italian heavily tainted with an Eastern accent. "I thought you might be indisposed for a while after our last meeting."

"No," the father replied. "You did an admirable job and, thanks to my strong constitution, the negative effects were quite brief."

The doctor peered into the other's mouth as he spoke.

"Yes. It's natural. Very natural."

"Eyes on the road please."

The car sped on, barely missing dogs, elderly women and baby carriages, crossed through the frontier without incident, their passports not so much as checked, and on into the wild countryside in the vicinity of Sežana. The dark, gnarled oaks sat near the edge of the road and, further on, past the thickly grassed meadows were the forests which rolled over the hills, rich and evergreen, a mask for prowling wolves. Off to one side was the ruined castle of Štanjel, the surrounding town like a horseshoe cast on the top of the low mountain, small vineyards, bereft of growth, levelling off into the valley below. The car wound up the road and through the portal of the bombed out watch-tower, the doctor violently sounding the horn as he made his way, at an extremely unsafe velocity, through the narrow opening. Then up, past the medieval church they went and through the narrow lane of mostly abandoned, gutted houses; the few that were inhabited having measly kitchen gardens in front, severe peasant women bent over ailing cabbages. The doctor lived at the far end of the village, in a refurbished villa with a courtyard.

"Ah, Žnidaršič!" he said affectionately, petting the slobbering dog that leaped on him as he got out of the car. Looking up at the priest, the dog's head sunk between its shoulder blades and it slunk off with a guilty expression, a low whine issuing from its mouth.

"Ah, Žnidaršič respects you," the doctor said. "It shows you are a powerful man. Animals sense that."

"It is a shame humans, generally speaking, do not."

The two men walked through the courtyard, which had a pine tree on one side, and an old well in the centre. Torturo plucked a few needles from the pine tree and stuck them in his pocket. Inside the villa, he was greeted by Nassa, the doctor's plump, blonde wife, who unfortunately did not speak a word of Italian.

"*Dobar dan, me veseli*," she said.

"She says she is glad to see you," the doctor translated with a smile, showing his fine white teeth. "She likes good business for her husband."

"Was she with you in America?" the father asked.

"No; I got her when I came back," the doctor replied seriously. "American women are no good. They don't like to work, or respect the husband. Life with Slovenian women is good. The women in America are no good. They call me criminal because I do good business."

"But you got caught in your 'good business.'"

"Life in America is like a mealy apple," the doctor said gravely. "It looks nice on the outside, but inside it is bad fruit. There some men who like to have funny things. They like the fetishes. Some like to have their legs sawed off. I am a good doctor, but if a weak man cannot live, it is not fair that I should get the blame. As you know, father, I am a very good doctor."

"Of course you are—That is why I am using you."

Nassa put down a plate of ham and freshly baked bread on the table, as well as an old Sprite bottle filled with black wine.

"Come," the doctor said motioning the priest to sit. "We eat and drink a glass of *teran*, the black wine, and then we do business. That is our custom you know; we always drink a glass of wine before business."

"An admirable custom," Father Torturo said as he watched his glass fill with the rich, dark liquid, the very blood of the earth.

"To your health."

"To your health."

The two men drank, each savouring the spectacular beverage. The doctor talked volubly, about wine, farming, his experiences as an unlicensed surgeon, and European politics. Torturo listened, or affected to listen, sipping gladly at his wine and every now and again slipping a bit of the delicious, fatty ham into his mouth. He found the doctor's physiognomy interesting: The large head, bristling with short, black hair; a small nose mounted above a ferocious moustache; the large, pink mouth, glowing with healthy teeth;—and then the eyes: soft, intelligent, almost feminine eyes! In some respects he reminded the priest of a great, trustworthy, clever dog.—In any case, the doctor certainly had two commendable qualifications: a definite quantity of mad genius, and enough self-interest to produce a moderate level of loyalty.

"Do you have eggs?" Torturo presently asked.

"Certainly. In the country we keep chickens, and they make good eggs; wholesome eggs. We consider our Slovenian eggs to be wholesome eggs. Would you like some?"

"Yes. One please."

"Fried, scrambled?"

"Hard-boiled."

Speaking rapidly the doctor instructed his wife to boil eggs. She complied without the least objection, apparently finding it quite natural to cook to order.

74

Father Torturo poured himself a fresh glass of wine and sat back, spilling the liquid into his mouth and letting it run over his tongue:—Or, in any case, the tongue that was in his mouth.

In 1263, when the vault containing the body of St. Anthony was opened, thirty-two years after its original internment, the flesh had turned to dust, but the tongue was in a perfect state of preservation, fresh and ripe as a red pepper. "O Blessed Tongue," St. Bonaventure had said, taking up the glossy morsel in two fingers and holding it high. "O Blessed Tongue that always praised the Lord, and made others bless Him, now it is evident what great merit thou hast before God."

Father Torturo, when he found himself in possession of this precious relic, the tongue of the man they called the *Malleus hereticorum*, the Hammer of the Heretics, was overjoyed. He filled a small mayonnaise jar with his own blood, draining it from an incision he made in his left palm, placed the tongue in the jar along with a silver amulet inscribed with the name Eresgichal written in Greek characters, sealed it and brought it with him on his first visit to Doctor Štrekel, who was less surprised at the priest's request than might be expected.

"Of course the thing might rot in your mouth," was his only objection.

"I have no fear on that score," Father Torturo had replied. "It has remained a healthy, living thing for nearly eight hundred years, so I imagine it can subsist a while longer rubbing against my palate."

"Oh, look how it wiggles in my fingers!" the doctor remarked, taking it out of the jar.

"Yes, it will graft beautifully. I have every confidence that it will graft beautifully."

The eggs were finished, and Father Torturo stuck one in his pocket. The two men, after draining their glasses of wine, walked across the wet courtyard, each carrying one of the suitcases, to the doctor's studio, which was not directly accessible from the house.

"Have you had much work since I last saw you?" Torturo asked, setting his luggage down on the floor.

The doctor shrugged his shoulders. "No, not much. Some nose jobs and one or two breast implants. One fellow came, nastily burned from a fire. I did a good skin graft. He had no money, so he paid me with a pig. We kill it soon and make good ham of the legs; nice roast of the loin.—Really though, that is about all. Not much work.—Not much work that's good for me." He grinned.

"Are you ever worried about botching a job? . . . Or, I should say: another job."

"Father, please," the doctor said with a hurt look on his large round face. "I was top student at the University of Leningrad. I am best surgeon. If I need confession I will come to you and trust you with my soul. So, as a personal favour, trust me in my job."

"You might trust me, in my capacity as priest, with your soul," the priest replied, "but I am trusting you with my body, which, here on earth, is often considered the more valuable of the two assets. But, believe me, I would not be using you if I judged you to be in the least bit incompetent."

"So, we set to work?"

"Certainly. Let me first just attend to a few matters—Alone."

"You want I should go?"

"If you don't mind—For three-quarters of an hour."

Left to himself, Torturo took the boiled egg from his pocket, cracked it on the edge of the table and peeled away its shell, leaving a glossy white oval in his palm. He set it down, took a penknife from the same pocket and pricked his thumb. Dipping the pine needle in the drop of blood, he wrote on the egg the word "*Adad*" and then, in a single swallow, took the hen's ovum into his stomach.

Clearing the work table of its contents, he drew on the whole, with a marker near at hand, a large circle. At each corner of the table he drew mystical symbols. Along the outer perimeter of the circle he wrote the twelve simple letters *héh, vau, zain, cheth, teth, yod, lamed, nun, samech, oin, tzaddi,* and *qoph*; along the inner perimeter he wrote the seven double letters *beth, gimel, daleth, kaph, peh, resh,* and *tau*. His hand worked fast and skilfully, without the least bit of hesitation. In the centre of the circle he wrote the word *ATzLH*.

He opened one of the suitcases. Inside were the incorrupt arms of Saint Ambrose, the metatarsals and phalanges of s.s. m.m. Naboree and Felice, the carpals of s.s. Gervaso and Protaso, and bones of St. Savina, St. Satio and St. Marcellina. He arranged the relics on the table and, waving his hand over them whispered a certain incantation, a certain formula bereft of sibilants.

The lights in the room wavered momentarily, and then turned slightly blue.

"*O'ôbôth yidde'onim*," he murmured.

There was a low hissing sound. A hazy film seemed to momentarily surround the table and a smell, like that of semen, filled the air. Torturo stood silent. Presently he bent down and placed the palms of his hands on the floor while keeping his knees locked. He arose, rolled his neck and then, stepping to the door and opening it, called to the doctor.

"Just coming," the latter said, who was in the court-yard playing catch with his dog. "Good boy, Žnidaršič! Good boy."

Torturo, inside, was unbuttoning his shirt.

The doctor went to the sink and proceeded to wash his hands. He looked over his shoulder, grinning, "You want that I should get the anaesthetic like before?— Little anaesthetic?"

"Yes. An anaesthetic would be fine."

"You are a fit fellow," the doctor said, admiring the priest's physique.

"I exercise and walk every day—I can hardly abide a day without walking."

"You walk much then?"

"A minimum of ten kilometres per day."

"You are a powerful man!"

"My body is earthly," said Torturo quietly. "Even animals like Žnidaršič suffer the pleasure of having one. My thoughts and reason on the other hand, as a human, should and do rest with God. There is kinship with the dead. There is kinship with the divine."

The doctor shrugged his shoulders. He dried his hands, cracked his knuckles and, picking up his scalpel, said, "Okay: we ate, we talk, we play: now we work."

❋

That afternoon Dr. Jure Štrekel performed a rather complex operation. Midway between the cephalic vein and radial nerve, he made an inch and a half wide incision, cutting cleanly through the epidermal tissue while carefully avoiding the musculature and lateral antibracheal cutaneous nerve beneath. By means not dissimilar to those used by the Jivaro Indians of Southern Ecuador, in the preliminary phases of producing a shrunken head, the bones of the arm were removed, leaving it a limp bag of flesh that resembled a large olive-coloured worm. To reassemble the framework, using humerus, radius and ulna foreign was the larger challenge. The cephalic vein was lifted with tenacula. Making use of the living gristle of his patient, Dr. Štrekel articulated the pulley-like trochlea, the distal end of the humerus to the ulna.

The doctor believed himself to be one of the most brilliant, though admittedly despised, medical men in the whole of Eastern Europe, and was more than willing to attempt the dangerous and tamper with the impossible. If he made a mutant, it would not be the first; if it was otherwise, then it would simply mean further prosperity, additional gold in his purse from the future operations the Italian priest had planned.

Doctor Štrekel was not timorous when it came to digging in open flesh, and feared not to go against either the laws of man or nature. That the spirits of

79

the dead inhabit not only the hollows of trees, dark forests, graveyards and rocks, but their very bones discarded of flesh is certain. The doctor was surprised at how smooth and rapid the operation proceeded. He worked with agility. Bones and bloody tissues sprang in his hands like sprightly, self-willed children. He was under the misapprehension that the work was all his own. He did not realise that there, in that village on the Slovenian border, in his own home, the supramundane had been invited.

VIII

IT was early morning and still dark out when young
Gianni stepped into Santa Giustina to pray, as was
his custom. He went to one of the pews near the front,
crossed himself, and then knelt down on one knee,
lowered his head and pressed his palms together. His
corral lips began to move, letting out low, sonorous
tones, and his handsome, slightly feline face took on
an angelic look. He was thoroughly abstracted in his
communion with the supreme being—too much so to
see the figure that had entered shortly after him and
lurked silently in the shadows.

Presently the figure stepped forward, moving slowly,
noiselessly, and worked its way around the nave, to the
pew immediately behind Gianni. It stopped, wavered
back and forth like a pliant tree in a breeze, and then
dramatically dropped to its knees and began to crawl
along the floor. The young acolyte raised his head,
looked around slightly and then settled back into
prayer. The figure paused for a few moments, and then
continued to creep along the pew, until directly behind
Gianni. The latter murmured a few words louder than

the rest. The figure rose up behind him and, producing a fuller's club from the folds of its garments, brandished it high.

Gianni, apparently sensing the presence, lifted and turned his head. It was at that moment that the first blow fell, with manic force. The skull cracked and re-sounded throughout the church, like a pitcher of wine falling on a parquet floor. Gianni did not so much as let out a cry. He collapsed to one side; his eyes swam toward the frescoed ceiling. The attacker leapt agilely over the pew and proceeded to rain blows on the boy, who instinctively lifted his arm to his face, but in no other way defended himself. His neck, ribs and sides were beaten mercilessly, while a foot pressed in on his stomach, making him vomit a series of pale pink bub-bles. The attacker kicked the acolyte's chin. A sudden resonance, booming, ringing, shot through the church.

The matins bells began to sound, and all Padua groan, forced to awake, forced away from simple sins and love making by these majestic cast iron contrivances.

The robed figure stepped backward out of the pew, dropped the club and, turning, hastily made its way through the side doors of the vestry. Gianni laboriously crawled the few feet it was from the nave to the aisle. His right hand caressed his own round face and, feel-ing the blood course down, over his left eye and cheek, traced the stream to its source: a giant fissure stretching from his forehead back. He looked at his vermilion hand, raised himself slightly and, trembling, traced a few letters on the floor before hiccoughing his final gore filled breath.

Seconds later a new figure emerged from behind a stone pillar, by the transept, and approached the body. It bent over; a hand felt the pulse, eyes gazed at the five letters written in blood. Spitting on a handkerchief, he wiped away the word.

※

Bishop Sebastiano Vivan sat at his desk, a magazine spread before him, with a dish of chocolate mousse to one side, which he was sensually spooning into his mouth as he read, a look of blissful ease on his face. There was a knock at the door.

"*Avanti!*" he said, looking up.

Father Torturo entered. His look was bold. His eyes were ringed with black.

"Do you have a spare moment?" he asked.

"Certainly, certainly," the bishop replied, licking mousse from his lips. "Please, have a seat."

The priest moved forward and sat down. His walk was noticeably lamed.

"What have you done, Torturo? You have hurt yourself!"

"Oh, it is nothing—I over-exerted myself while exercising, that is all."

"Poor man!" cried Vivan. "You take this bodily training too far."

"And you—you eat far too many dainties."

Vivan blushed. He sucked his bottom lip.

"I see you are enjoying further literature," the father said presently.

"Yes," Vivan replied, closing the copy of *Boy's Life* magazine and turning the cover in Torturo's direction. "I have a subscription from America. The English is very difficult, but the pictures are, er;—let us say the pictures inspire me. They speak about modes of a pure life: A child's life with nature. They tell of lads, innocent fellows, and their adventures—their humid adventures in forests, and on the rocky shores of North American lakes . . . To see a young man vigorously clasping a rod, a fishing rod; or bending over and thrusting a stake into the earth, a tent stake: Really, it is one of the most beautiful things."

"Children are unquestionably interesting."

"They are fascinating."

"Particularly the boys of the species."

"Absolutely the boys."

"Did the police come and question you?"

"Question me? Well, naturally. I saw Gianni on an almost daily basis. It was a tragedy. I sent his mother a pot of orchids (charming flowers). I hope you will be there for the services, father. Your presence would be appreciated."

"Of course I will go. He was, as you say, a charming boy."

"Charming in the extreme."

"And do the police have any suspects?"

"None that they have indicated—though they say there might be a connection between this and the other murder—the one that happened a month or two back."

"I suspect that there is such a connection."

"There could be," Vivan said with a sigh, his eyes straying heavenward; and then, bringing them down and steadily fixing them on Father Torturo. "There are unfortunately a great many evils in this world."

"True. It is some consolation that Gianni died like a saint."

"I don't quite follow you," Vivan said with a gentle, consolidating smile.

"Like Saint Peter of Verona, to be exact," Torturo grinned. "Remember the words '*Credo in Deem*'?"

Vivan raised his eyebrows questioningly.

"As you know," Torturo continued, "good Peter was walked from Como to Milan one evening, the sixth of April 1252 to be exact. In the forest around Cesano a Manichæan named Carino jumped him and split his head open with an axe. Peter, half dead, rose to his knees and recited the first article of the Symbol of the Apostles. Dipping his fingers in his own blood, he offered it as a sacrifice to God. Using it as ink, he wrote on the ground '*Credo in Deem*.' Carino then jammed a blade into his heart."

"Yes, yes yes," Vivan said with a wave of his hand. "And the body was carried to Milan where it was entombed in an ark at Sant' Eustorgio, where it remained until the tragic event three weeks ago. I understand all this, but what connection does it bare to our dear departed Gianni?"

"Why, it is apparent that Gianni, in his last moments was inspired by Peter, the martyr of Verona."

"Inspired? How?"

"Gianni also managed to jot down a few letters."

85

"Pardon?"

"Before he died, he wrote a name on the floor. In his own blood."

Bishop Vivan's boyish face flushed bright scarlet. He pursed and then licked his lips and then swallowed. His clear green eyes became extraordinarily wide as he looked at the father and asked, "And . . . and whose name was it that was written?"

"Why, the murderer's of course."

"The murderer?" Vivan gasped.

"Yes. Why look so shocked? The murderer;—the same man I saw clobber poor Gianni with a fuller's club as I stood hidden in the transept. It was a remarkably cruel act. I knew you had certain vicious instincts in you, bishop, but I must admit that, until I saw you at work I never suspected you of such absolute heinousness. I suppose, until then, I took you for an ordinary pervert . . . But honestly, the look in your eyes as you slew him was beyond nasty."

The bishop rose from his seat, his countenance glowing with guilty indignation. "How dare you say such things," he shouted. And then, lowering his voice, "How can you say I did it? I didn't. I didn't, I tell you. I loved Gianni!"

"I do not have a doubt in the world that you loved the lad," Father Torturo said calmly, taking a pack of cigarettes and matches from his pocket. "You loved him, not as Jesus loved his enemies and blessed those who cursed him, but as Othello loved, your love voluptuous and mixed with a zest for blood. You loved him as you loved young Baldasari Sorrissi. That's right;

don't think I never saw Baldo entering your office at odd hours—Or, for that matter, leaving it in a state of disarray. I fancy you had been seeing him since he was a boy?"

"Well, I used to be his confessor, years ago—but that is no reason to imply——"

"I am implying nothing," the father said, raising his voice. "I am saying that you are a swine and a criminal of the lowest order; the stereotypical Catholic degenerate!" Resuming his calm demeanour, he put a cigarette between his lips and proceeded to light it.

"I . . . I don't allow smoking in my chambers," Vivan stuttered.

"Be quiet," Father Torturo said brusquely. "You work for me now. You will do as I say or pay the consequences."

"You would turn me in to the authorities?"

"Certainly."

"Well, there are worse things than being despised in the eyes of men."

"Are there?"

"I . . . I have heard it said that there are."

"And your mother? Your dear old mother? What will she think when I tell her, with a pitying look on my face, of her son's morbid homosexuality, of his stabbing a boy with a knife nineteen times (along with the psychosexual implications), of the other lad, your office boy, and how you cracked open his skull in the very house of the Lord? Do you fancy she will be proud of the disgrace you have brought upon the Church?"

"Mother!" Vivan cried, collapsing in his seat, tears bursting from his shy green eyes. "She thinks I am such a good boy. I would rather have a red-hot iron shoved down my throat than have her find out."

"Then I am your iron," Father Torturo said, taking a long and forceful drag of his cigarette, as if he were drinking thirst quenching liquid instead of inhaling a slow acting poison. "You will do what I ask of you and, in the end, find yourself in a better position than ever—Your mother will be given but further reason to be proud of you, her loyal and dulcet son."

Vivan took out a handkerchief and began to dab at his eyes. "So," he said. "So, you will not tell on me?"

"No. Not if you do as I say."

"Well . . . Well, then I will," Vivan murmured, his face taking on a set, businesslike expression. And then, smiling, "But please; treat me well. I am rather sensitive, as you can see, and damage under rough handling."

IX

IT was a grey day in Venice. The man peered through his sunglasses as the boat passed St. Mark's and the Palazzo Ducale, with its knots of pigeon feeding fools and pairs of floundering tourists out front, inebriated by the foul lagoon air. He got off the boat at San Zaccaria, being careful, as he stepped, not to soil his white linen suit. His legs set off in rigid, determined strides down the Calle Albenesi, past the Prigioni. By his dress and his rather severe countenance, an onlooker would have taken him for some well-to-do German tourist or art collector—possibly an author; certainly not a plebeian. He looked at his watch, saw that it was a quarter past four in the afternoon, and doubled his pace. It was obvious that he had an appointment which he was eager to keep. He moved rapidly along the Calle Sagresita, in three sweeping steps crossed the Rio di San Giovanni Novo, turned up Ruga Giuffa, and, after negotiating a few minute back lanes, strode down an alley that came to a dead end at the Rio di San Formosa, the dark water splashing against the stone embankment where a small motor boat was moored. There was an undersized wooden door to his left, worn and patched, with a few flakes of green paint still adhering to it, the original coat of which must have been added to the antique portal at least fifty years previous. One of his long bony fingers stretched out and pressed against an electric bell with the name "Sig. C. Della Casa" written beneath it. Taking a handkerchief from his jacket pocket, he wiped his forehead and waited, gently stroking a mouse that crawled out from the cave of his sleeve.

Twenty minutes later the man was stripped to his socks and underwear, on his hands and knees in the interior of the apartment. A woman, Signora Clara Della Casa, stood over him, wearing knee-high leather boots, red lace panties, and a black latex top, which was cut low enough to reveal the majority of a swelling balcony. The windowless room was lit by a single phosphorescent bulb enwrapped in a red Chinese lantern which hung overhead. The steady surge of house music, a four-on-the-floor beat, pulsed from the stereo, adding a sense of youthful urgency to the scene.

Clara cracked a three-tasselled whip over his buttocks.

"Now," she said, standing hip-shot, arms akimbo, her large cellulose thighs swelling majestically; "will you be obedient, slave?"

"Yes, yes," he whimpered gleefully.

She cracked the whip dangerously near his left ear.

"Yes, what?" she cried.

"Yes, Mistress. I will do anything you say, Mistress."

"Kneel! You hear me, doggy?—kneel!"

He sat back on his haunches, revealing a thin, bird-like chest thickly covered with grey hair. He posed his hands like a puppy and looked up at her, his eyes glassy with subservient lust.

"Stick out your tongue."

He complied, letting the wet red organ hang from his mouth. His head was hot and glands well stoked. He crawled forward.

"Lick me;—Lick me here!" she demanded.

✳

"I think we have enough now Clara, thank you."

"What the hell," the cardinal cried, wheeling around.

"You were magnificent," Bishop Vivan smiled, capping the lense on the video camera.

Both himself and Father Torturo were dressed in civilian clothes, Vivan looking particularly spry in close-fitting black pants and shirt by Max Mara, and a pair of brown leather loafers which he wore without socks.

"Vivan, is that you? My God——"

"With Father Torturo. You remember him, right?"

The cardinal rose to his feet, his face beginning to take on the colours of an eggplant. "I . . . I . . . I am," he stuttered incoherently. And then, his lips quivering: "I am confessing her," he gasped.

"Yes," Torturo said suavely, "I can see you are dressed appropriately for the occasion. Do you like his vestments?" he asked, turning to Vivan.

"Oh, very much! Very much indeed! And really, for his age, his figure is not half bad."

"*Fava della Madonna!*" the cardinal screamed, white with rage, and clenched his fists. "Vivan, what the devil are you doing here?"

"I might just as easily ask you the same question," the bishop replied coolly with one hand on his hip.

"And, so I would guess, your answer would be less than satisfactory," Torturo added, taking a pack of cigarettes from his pocket.

"May I have one?" Clara asked, setting down her whip and stepping towards the priest.

"Certainly; but please put something on over those hips and latex. They are liable to distract the cardinal and we have business to discuss."

"Would you rather I leave for a while?"

"That might be better," he said, handing her a cigarette and three hundred euro notes. "Go down to the bar and get something to drink, on me. Come back in half an hour or forty-five minutes. We should be all settled up here by then. And cardinal," he continued, lighting a match for Clara and then applying the flame to his own cigarette, "you might slip something on as well. Our good bishop is rather too generous with his compliments. Take it from me, a few weeks unsheathed in the sun and a regular program of callisthenics would do you a world of good. As it is, I feel like I am looking at the thin wedge of fat around a joint of prosciutto."

"Listen, priest," the cardinal said, showing the very gums of his teeth, "I don't know what your game is, but you will surely suffer for crossing me."

"As I have already indicated," Torturo said, exhaling a jet of smoke, "seeing you thus I take to be a rather trying punishment. Please be so kind as to put on your trousers."

"You can't blackmail me!"

"I can."

"It won't stick."

"It will."

"And if I don't comply? If I don't care about my reputation?"

Father Torturo's lips became set. The cigarette dropped from his fingers. "Then," he said in a menacing voice that rose into a violent crescendo. "Then," he said, reaching into his pocket. "Then I will make you suffer twice what you deserve—And, like this damn mouse, dash the life out of your tedious, bloodless carcass!" He raised the white, squirming handful over his head and flung it brutally to the floor, where it let out a horrible squeak and then lay, quite broken, its little mouth agape, showing minuscule teeth set in pink lips.

"Picolito!" the cardinal cried, throwing himself down beside the mouse. He took it in his hands and pressed it, a lifeless rodent, to his face. He looked up at the priest with a horrified expression, crying, "You are a madman; a scoundrel; a cruel maniac!"

Torturo stood, powerful, immobile, unsympathetic. Vivan simpered, though his face showed signs of emotion.

"*Ciao*," Clara called, walking out the front door, dressed in leather slacks and a turtle-neck sweater. "You boys have fun!"

"Vivan, lock the door behind her," Father Torturo said. And, looking coldly at the cardinal: "Put on your clothes."

Zuccarelli was visibly shaken. Alone, in a locked apartment with two men whose program seemed to be so diametrically opposed to his own left his mouth empty of the demands and cutting remarks he was habituated to spill forth. He lifted his shirt and white linen suit from the chair upon which they had been flung and, without a word more of opposition, stepped into the bathroom to dress.

"Would you like wine, coffee, tea?" Vivan asked, sliding towards the kitchen, the front door key bouncing in his hand.

"Coffee," Torturo replied

A quarter of an hour later all three men were seated in the living room, sipping the espresso which Vivan had prepared.

"Today is your lucky day," Torturo said to Zuccarelli. "I am sure that my methods have led you to believe that I intend you harm, when, in fact, nothing could be further from the truth. My intentions are to better your situation, by a rather broad margin. Don't look so disgusted, signore, I am being sincere."

"And I am sincere in my disgust. Do you think I could be otherwise after your intrusion into my private affairs with a video camera? Do you think I could trust a man whose aim is so obviously the destruction of my pleasures?"

"A certain English authoress once wrote that the pleasantness of an employment does not always evince its propriety. Now, that you find pleasure from paying Clara to let you suck her toes and feel the point of her heel, I feel no doubt. But, for a man in your position such a thing is certainly viewed as an impropriety. Now I personally," (with a carefree gesture of his hand). "I personally have nothing against such hobbies, and am willing to give you full indulgence. Is all I ask for in return is your co-operation."

"Listen to him," Vivan said sweetly, sipping his coffee. "His offer is really not a bad one."

"What exactly is his offer?" Zuccarelli asked, somewhat pacified now that the scene had taken on a more businesslike tone.

"To begin with," Torturo said, "I want, I require a cardinalature."

"Absurd!" Zuccarelli laughed grotesquely.

"I agree," Torturo responded. "It is absurd. It still, however, would give me a certain measure of worldly satisfaction."

"I don't doubt that in the least. I am sure you would be quite satisfied. But I don't see that I am the man to grant it. Only the Pope can make a cardinal, and I do not see, even if I were to put in a good word for you, that he would be inclined to make such a gift. These things are done, to a certain measure, for services rendered."

"Oh, don't worry on that score," Torturo remarked casually. "I will render services."

X

THE pig had been hanging from the pine tree since morning, its hind legs secured to a branch by a rope. The doctor kicked Žnidaršič away from the pool of blood, cut the pig down and heaved its body into the centre of the court, near the well, onto the flagstones warmed by the sun.

"This is good wholesome meat," he murmured as he began to carve the pig.

The dog barked.

"Žnidaršič! Žnidaršič!" the doctor called.

A man, probably in his mid-thirties, though with relatively boyish features, walked in. It was Marco. The dog ceased barking, approached Marco, and licked his hand and he, in turn, petted the dog

"I was looking for a Dr. Štrekel," he said, approaching the doctor.

"Ah; and what do you need with him?"

"I was told—I was told by a friend of mine that he could—That he could," (grinning weakly). "Well . . . I was told that he could help me fulfil a certain urge."

"An urge, eh?" the doctor said, still leaning intently over his work and only glancing up.

"Yes. I—I often think of spikes. Spikes and tusks. Pogo sticks, cucumbers and carrots.—Really I do need to be;—I do think of tusks so often!"

The doctor looked at Marco archly. "Really?" he said.

"Really. Much too often."

"So—you think of tusks?"

"Yes. My general practitioner laughed when I told him what I wanted. He did not understand . . . I need someone who will do it for me."

"Do it?"

"Yes.—Cut it off. Cut the left one off. I want the left one cut off."

"Are you serious?" The doctor's intelligent eyes darted up and met Marco's.

"I have never been more serious. I have money and will pay. I want the left one removed."

"You have money and need some good work done, eh? . . . Well; then I suppose I am your man. Dr. Jure Štrekel at your service!" The doctor lifted up his hands. They were dripping with blood, the grim entrails of the pig hanging out of one clenched fist, like a macabre garland. "Ha!" he laughed, displaying his large, pink mouth and sparkling teeth. "I have been operating on this pork!—But come inside, I wash up and we talk things over."

Marco followed the doctor inside, the dog trotting at their heels. Nassa was in the kitchen, kneading dough. The doctor spoke a few words to her in Slovenian and she walked out of the room, inclining her head slightly towards Marco as she went.

"So, what friend told you of me," the doctor asked, rinsing his hands in the sink.

"A friend;—an acquaintance of mine . . . A priest."

"Ah, the Father Torturo was it?"

"Yes. He is my intimate friend."

"Then that is good. He is an honest man.—We drink wine and discuss business. It is better to talk business over wine."

"Certainly," Marco agreed. "It might help me overcome my embarrassment.—I have never done anything like this before!"

The doctor turned around and walked towards the cabinets, talking volubly as he did so about the quality of his *teran*, his "black wine." Marco felt the pistol, which was equipped with a silencing device, in his jacket pocket and stepped behind the doctor. The doctor opened the cabinet, bent down, and reached for a plastic Sprite bottle, full of dark liquid. Marco slipped the gun from his pocket.

"My wife will bring the prosciutto," the doctor said, slowly rising. "We eat and drink a glass of the black wine, and then do business." Unscrewing the top of the bottle, and lifting it to his nose: "That is our custom, you know; we always drink a glass of wine before business."

"A good custom," Marco said while placing the barrel of the gun a few inches from the back of the doctor's head, and pulling the trigger. Without so much as letting out a cry, the man fell forward, slamming the cabinet door shut and then toppling to the floor. The open bottle dropped from his hand. A circle of blood leisurely expanded around him and mixed with the black wine, which flowed fluidly.

Marco heaved a sigh. His arms hung limp at his sides. Žnidaršič licked his right hand, which still held the gun, and then began to lap at the pool of blood.

Nassa, the doctor's plump, blonde wife walked in carrying a plate of ham and a loaf of home-baked bread which she set on the table. She smiled stiffly, cautiously at Marco. The only sound in the room was that of the dog, lapping away. Marco looked at her sadly, tenderly. Her own gaze dropped to the floor, where it fell upon the body of her husband swimming in gore. She shrieked, loudly and frantically, threw her arms in front of her face and staggered back. Marco lifted the pistol, bit his bottom lip, and shot her twice in the neck. She reeled against a wall and fell, sliding down, her legs sprawled. He approached the quivering body and dispatched a third bullet into her crown. Žnidaršič turned and barked, alarmed at the noise, which was like a melon dropped on the floor. The dog received its death, a bullet being sent into its head with cold precision.

The young man dragged the woman's body into the courtyard, a clear trail of blood streaking the flagstones behind her. He lifted the temperate corpse to the opening of the well, and threw it in. The doctor was quite heavy. His mouth was open and his white teeth shone in a set smile. Marco managed, with great effort, to drag him to the well. Straining himself, he worked the heavy frame over the stone edge and watched it topple into the black hole. Žnidaršič he threw in after, and then walked back into the house and washed his hands in the sink, with hot water and soap. After drying his hands with a paper towel, he approached the table, stepping gingerly over the pool of blood. The loaf of bread, *treccia*, braided white bread glazed with egg, sat on a cutting board. A fly buzzed around the plate of ham, and alighted on a white spot of fat. Marco shooed it away, picked up a piece of the ham and ate it, slowly and despondently.

"It is really quite good prosciutto," he murmured.

XI

BEFORE sending Marco to conduct the afore-mentioned business with Dr. Štrekel, Torturo had made sure that he was through with his services. The doctor had, within half a dozen surgical sessions, given the priest those miraculous relics of the saints to keep encased in his own living muscle and meat. In between operations Torturo had stretched his limbs and exercised incessantly. He ate restorative foods: tripe soup, wild pheasant and boiled marrow bones. Oils of myrrh and frankincense he rubbed on his wounds, and the proper incantations he muttered thrice daily, taking care to perform all the necessary articles of his practice.

The priest who Vivan had once described as "inoffensive as an insect" was rapidly coming into his own. That he had very little in common with a buzzing, two-winged insect was now openly apparent. He had subjugated Vivan with ease. Zuccarelli could not be said to have been subjugated, but the man had clearly seen that to help Torturo was in his own best interest.

Both men wondered about this priest, this well-built man in his thirties who chain-smoked Parisiennes and who, apparently, had as deep and dark a clandestine life as could be imagined. Rumours had been floating about for some weeks that he was occasionally visited by the Holy Ghost. He had been seen entering a cheese shop during a torrential rain, every inch of him completely dry. At the intersection of the via Benedetto Cairoli and the via Jacopo Avanzo a bus had run over a seven-year-old boy's foot. Torturo instantly appeared upon the scene, pushed the hysterical mother aside and, after removing the boy's shoe, rubbed his foot. The child laughed, rose to his feet and danced along the sidewalk.

One night Torturo was preaching on the nature of the spirit world at Il Santo. Vivan was a member of the audience and was both impressed and moved by the oratory. Zuccarelli walked in and approached him.

"Who is that?" he whispered.

"Father Torturo—his voice is like wild honey."

"Impossible!"

"You don't like wild honey?"

"Not the honey, idiot! The notion that that is Torturo—it cannot be him."

"And why is that?"

"Because on my way here I passed by the Church of Eremitani. Torturo was there contemplating the half decimated fresco by Mantegna of the annunciation of the virgin. We talked for thirty minutes."

"But I have been sitting here intoxicated by his voice for three-quarters of an hour!" Vivan said, his eyes growing wide with astonishment.

"*Fava de la Madonna*," Zuccarelli murmured. "Our priest is a mesmerist."

Not long after this incident, a young nun claimed that, while she slept, Torturo visited and admonished her for aberrant thoughts. "He, in the likeness of sinful flesh, and for sin, condemned sin in the flesh!" She insisted that the man would do great things in the Church.

"So now you are you working miracles?" Bishop Vivan asked him one day with a silly, self-conscious smile.

"The miracles of one age become the commonplace workings of nature in the next," Torturo replied simply.

Through the efforts of Vivan and Zuccarelli, he was made an auxiliary bishop of Padua.

When he appeared before the cardinal with a suitcase full of bones and a jar containing a tongue the latter became apprehensive.

"What do we have here?" he asked.

"The tongue of Saint Anthony and the relics of Milan."

"And how did you come by them?"

"As an official statement?"

"I suppose it had better be," Zuccarelli replied nervously.

"Officially: I prayed and fasted. I recited the responsory of Friar Julian of Spires: *Si quaeris miracula; resque perditas*. A messenger was put before me. As I knelt, behold, then an angel touched me, and said 'Arise, I will show thee where they be.' Then we walked to and fro over the earth and through the myrtles. The place where the relics were hidden was revealed in a vision."

"And where was that?"

"In the hollow of a fig tree near Limena."

"You fetched them?"

"I did."

"And this story is to be believed?"

"It will be accepted. Us Catholics, after all, are not without faith;—We are not materialists."

Zuccarelli drew up a statement, outlining Torturo's story and adding his own conviction that it was so. Vivan lent his signature to the document and it was sent to Cardinal O'Malley, one of the key figures in Rome and a man on politically intimate terms with Zuccarelli. O'Malley, through partial coercion, managed to see a number of other signatures of prominent men affixed to the document, including those of the Archbishop of Milan and the Cardinal-Bishop of Ostia. The Vatican, though pleased with the news, refused to offer its sanction to the relics without a verification procedure. A meeting was called of numerous ecclesiastic authorities, in order to ascertain the validity of the relics.

"I do not know whose tongue that is over there on the table and, frankly, I do not want to know," Zuccarelli said in a low voice, as the various ecclesiastics gathered in the Palazzo della Ragione in Padua. "Outwardly I will remain convinced that it is the tongue of Saint Anthony;—I have told you I would do so much, and I will. Over my inner feelings, however, you have no jurisdiction."

"Oh, you don't need to lay bare your heart to me Cardinal," Torturo replied. "I am perfectly satisfied with outward pretence."

"And you shall have it;—from me. But remember, we are not alone. The men you see around you, for the most part, are not fools. Though I have my supporters here, I also have my enemies. When I say something is true, they will surely claim it to be false."

"Yes, Cardinal Gonzales, who has been warming himself in front of the fireplace, has been giving you a most unpleasant look for the last five minutes."

"I noticed. It is because I am intimate with O'Malley, whose interests are opposed to his own. He does not dare offend the man personally, because he is afraid of him. It is much more convenient for him to display his impertinence towards myself, whom he considers harmless."

"Yet I imagine there are more fitting adjectives to describe you."

"Thank you—I suppose."

"They have closed the doors. I presume we are ready to begin?"

"Yes; to our seats."

The various members of the committee found their seats around the great wooden table placed in the centre of the room, with cassocks fluttering and whispers exchanged. In the middle of the table was a small golden casket, lined with white silk, on which sat the tongue; to one side sat a larger casket containing the relics of Milan. A few old ecclesiastics sniffed at the tongue and poked through the bones.

Zuccarelli, who was to head the committee, sat at one end of the table, Gonzales, an agile old cardinal, at the other. All the chief ecclesiastics from Padua were there, including of course Vivan, and many from Rome. Torturo took his place next to Cardinal Di Quaglio, a plump, polite little man with smooth white hands and a double chin. The latter's nostrils widened. He looked over at Torturo.

"Excuse me," he whispered, "but what is that cologne you're wearing? It smells categorically celestial!"

Torturo smiled stiffly and shrugged his shoulders.

Zuccarelli opened the meeting with a brief speech outlining the general circumstances and stated that he firmly believed that the relics were genuine and should be seen as such. Gonzales roundly objected, stating that there was little more evidence that they were real than the word of a single priest.

"Are you calling him a liar?" Zuccarelli asked pointedly.

Gonzales pursed his lips. "I make no direct accusations," he said.

"And where do you propose he got the bones from?"

"We are in Italy;—bones are far from rare."

"And the tongue?"

Gonzales gave the ghost of a smile. "Oh, men lose their tongues often enough."

A number of those present burst out in indignation. The comment was generally taken to be in poor taste.

Torturo stood up before the assembly. He seemed to almost glow in the ill-lit room. There was a certain bearing, a power to his person which was ineffable. He exuded, not only supreme self-confidence, but a kind of dominant strength that was somewhat uncanny.

"Cardinal Gonzales has kindly informed us that men often lose their tongues," he said, "while giving us a brief but piquant demonstration that he has not lost his own."

"The fellow certainly does have fire," thought Zuccarelli. "It is remarkable that he remained unknown to me for so long. We could have been of use to each other earlier."

Torturo placed his fingertips on the table and continued: "My veracity has been brought into question: The dead bodies of thy servants have they given to be meat unto the fowls of the heaven, the flesh of thy saints unto the beasts of the earth.—Now, let us be clear about the matter at hand: We have before us right relics of the saints, and, according to the Council of Trent, we must pay them due respect.—The holy bodies of holy martyrs, which bodies were the living members of Christ and the temple of the Holy Ghost and which are by Him to be raised to eternal life and to be glorified are to be venerated by the faithful, for through these many benefits are bestowed by God on men.—Furthermore, Vivan is the bishop of this diocese and he has recognised the relics as authentic."

"Yes," Vivan said with a simper. "I know a relic when I see one and those are relics;—That tongue looks awfully relic to me."

"It is all very well to talk randomly on these matters," Gonzales said peevishly, the loose skin which hung from his chin to his throat, like that of a lizard, quivering, "but, the fact is that the bishop is required to obtain accurate information, to take council with theologians and pious men, and in cases of doubt or exceptional difficulty to submit the matter to the sentence of the metropolitan and other bishops of the province. Furthermore, nothing new, or that previously has not been usual in the Church, shall be resolved on, without having first consulted the Holy See."

"That is the very process which we are engaged in," Zuccarelli said solemnly. "And I suggest we go about it respectfully. We must hold in the highest regard the saints who were so much beloved by God, and also their bones, which were once the frameworks of the temples of the Holy Ghost."

"But these are mere bones!" Gonzales burst out in disgust. "Possibly those of some worthless beggar—And God only knows where the tongue came from! Bishop Quivil of Exeter, whose authority on the matter is pronounced, clearly states that relics should in no way be venerated on account of dreams or on fictitious grounds."

"Cardinal Gonzales," Torturo said coolly, "you seem determined to cast a doubting shadow over this assembly. What you refer to as 'mere bones' are more precious than refined gold;—The tongue is a priceless treasure.—I do not have the least doubt that, were you shown Saint Peter's chains, you would say they were for tires in snow and, were your eyes exposed to the gridiron of Saint Laurence, you would claim it was meant for the pressing of waffles.—Bishop Quivil, in making that statement (which you so kindly abridged)

108

was referring to the discovery of *new* relics;—He in no way intended it to be used in regard to the *re-discovery* of relics already regarded as such."

These words won Torturo general approval, but all those present were still by no means convinced. One old and much respected ecclesiastical scholar rose to his feet and spoke.

"Though I do not for a single moment doubt the good father's credibility and I admit his story sounds plausible when looked at from a purely Catholic point of view, I still feel some reservations in admitting this to be the authentic tongue of Saint Anthony. In the history of the Church there have been many unfortunate occurrences where spurious relics have been introduced. Though I would like to believe that this is the genuine article, and have the right and proper tongue of Saint Anthony restored to its sanctified home, my conscious still cries out for proof. Where is the proof, my friends?"

There was a murmur throughout the room. All eyes were on the tongue. Many brows were furrowed. Minds were hesitant upon which way to turn. Zuccarelli, perplexed, bit his bottom lip and looked at Torturo, as if to say, "There, now the ball's in your court."

Torturo bent forward and, with a rapid yet suave gesture grabbed up the tongue, turned around and cast it into the fire. Every man, as if attached to a single spring rose to their feet in an uproar. All bodies rushed towards the fire, all arms stretched towards the flames. Torturo, powerful, magnificent, with arms wide and legs spread, barred the way.

"No!" he cried. "Stand back you of miniature faith! If God cannot speak through your hearts, let him speak through the flames!"

"But you'll burn it!" Vivan cried.

Most everyone in the room begged Torturo to step aside, a few even attempting to use physical force, but the priest, with an almost ecstatic look on his face, held them back. Many pulled their hair and wrung their hands in despair—for that the tongue was genuine the majority of the party had already been convinced. To have the relic once more in their possession only to be deprived of it, and this time without hope of ever seeing it returned, was horrible.

Some suggested calling in the carabinieri and having the priest arrested.

"You are a madman!" one cardinal sputtered, looking at Torturo with wild, bloodshot eyes.

"I seem to have heard that comment before," the other replied with just the slightest hint of a smile playing on his lips. "But, if I am a madman, then surely I am one who lives amongst maniacs." He stooped over the fire and, with an iron poker, fished through the burning bits of timber and hot coals, which sent up sprays of gem-like sparks. Delicately, with two fingers, he pinched what appeared to be a live coal from the fire, and turned. "I simply have faith," he said raising the tongue up high, unharmed, red and ripe as a strawberry. "It has fulfilled its just probation, has it not?"

There was a murmur of general astonishment. The perfume of the supernatural struck every man's nostrils. None dared contest such evidence. Torturo set the tongue back in its casket and strode out of the room, victorious.

"I will break down the barriers," he murmured to himself. "This body of flesh is all simply an instrument; let me fit it out properly. I myself must be as God, because God created me, as a spider does his web;—I cannot be denied my just inheritance. My desires are, after all, not evil;—I only wish to promote general and universal . . . welfare."

Four days later Cardinal Zuccarelli sat in his private office, filling out the paperwork required for Torturo's nomination for cardinal.

"Will Torturo be pliant?" O'Malley had asked him.

"Pliant?—Possibly.—But one thing is certain: It is better to work with him than against him. I firmly believe he can help us forward our own aims."

"Then I will send you over the paperwork and we'll see what we can do for the lad."

O'Malley had the complete confidence of the Vatican. He was the pronuncio, one of the key figures in the process of selecting new cardinals and continually strove to keep the balance of power tilted in his direction.

"*Please describe the nature of your association with the candidate and indicate the length of time that you have known him,*" Zuccarelli read aloud from the questionnaire.

He speedily scribbled out several paragraphs of well-turned lies.

Question: *What human qualities does the candidate have?*

Answer: *He is endowed with a remarkable degree of both speculative and practical intellectual capacity; his temperament and character are evenly balanced; he is serene of judgment; has an almost overpowering sense of responsibility.*

Question: *What are the candidate's human, Christian and priestly formations?*

Answer: *He is possessed of all human, Christian and priestly virtues, i.e. prudence, justice, moral uprightness, loyalty, sobriety, faith, hope, charity, obedience, humility, piety: daily celebration of the Eucharist and of the Liturgy of the Hours, Marian devotion.*

Question: *What is the candidate's behaviour?*

Answer: *He conducts himself with moral exactitude; his comportment with people in general and in the exercise of the priestly ministry in particular is upright in the highest degree; he is endowed with the rare ability to establish friendships in the most diverse corners; he is respected by and in perfect rapport with civil authorities.*

Torturo was successfully appointed, along with twenty-eight other new cardinals. The ceremony was grand. Torturo showed himself to be modest and a man of commendable manners. At the Vatican he was well received. His days of obscurity appeared to be at an end.

XII

UPON receiving the news that the tongue had been restored to its rightful place, in the Basilica del Santo, the world rejoiced. Pilgrims in unprecedented quantities came from every continent and country to view the miraculous bit of flesh, first filling the hotels beyond capacity and then spilling out onto the streets of Padua, where they milled and moved with bovine facility. Under the recommendation of the city fire department, special guards were set up at the doors of the basilica with instructions to only allow a specified number of visitors in at a time. The number of pilgrims rapidly multiplied and soon they were requested to call ahead for reservations. The lines of people levelled off onto the via Capelli, where traffic was blocked. On several occasions the police were called in to control the mob, which periodically threatened to become violent. At one point an American man, far from lean in his proportions and wielding a camera menacingly over his head, made statements to a priest, the purport of which could not be mistaken.

"I have been here since eight o'clock this morning," the man shouted (it was then eleven). "You sons of bitches have been ignoring my reservation! Is this how you treat American citizens!"

A number of his compatriots joined in, raising their voices high above the noise of the crowd, and, from what could be understood, demanded either entrance or sacerdotal blood. In the weeks that followed, similar outbursts were heard from groups of Germans, English, Danish and Irish. It was decided that those visitors willing to make a moderate donation of twenty euros would be allowed carte blanche status. A considerable sum was thus gathered, only about sixty percent of which found its way into the pocket of Bishop Vivan and, in turn, Cardinal Torturo. It was, after all, his tongue the people were paying to see.

Meanwhile the other relics, that is Torturo's femurs, fibulas, tibias, etc, were transported to Rome, where they were to be specially exhibited in the Vatican before being returned to their rightful home in Milan. The responsibility for promoting the event was handed over to the Italian Board of Tourism who, with their usual skill in attracting attention to the most splendid country on earth, did a marvellous job. Full page ads were taken out in all the leading Catholic newspapers, as well as the travel sections of both the New York Times and the London Guardian. The Italian Prime Minister, perfectly aware of the percentage of the profits he would gain, loaned his vast media-conglomeration-network to the exploitation of the restored relics at home, taking the line that it was, more or less, every Italian's duty to view these emblems of their nation's spiritual and cultural heritage. The admission to this magnificent display was a mere ten euros.

The Pope, who was to be the first to see the line-up, arrived some three-quarters of an hour late. He shuffled along the range of glass cases in which the relics were elaborately displayed, placed on gold-trimmed velvet and lit with a subtle, somewhat mysterious light placed in such a way as to give the impression that it exuded from the bones themselves. Over the cases were placed old master paintings by such artists as Botticelli, Signorelli and Raphael, which, due to the fact that they were put in a subordinate position, heightened the implied value of the human remains. The old man's eyes, glassy and bespeaking an entire absence of strength, passed over the bones which were before him, his vague expression seeming to say: "Oh, you lucky dogs; look how you rest!"

"The man is sublime," Cardinal Gonzales, who was following close behind His Holiness in order to catch him if he fell, whispered to Di Quaglio.

"The Pope wobbles," Di Quaglio muttered to Cardinal O'Malley, who was close at hand.

"Then let him wobble," O'Malley replied, his thin Irish lips curling slightly.

Di Quaglio slipped his arm through that of Gonzales, holding him back in order to point out his admiration for the thigh bone of Saint Satio. The Pope shuffled on ahead, trembling. There was a gathering in the red velvet rug. Naturally the Pope's foot, which never rose above three-eighths of an inch from floor level, contacted the said gathering. He tripped. His head collided with the side of the glass case and he fell to the ground. There was only a very small gash above his left eyebrow, but the man was dead.

The sensation was tremendous. All the bells in Rome were rung. Merchants closed their shops; field workers lay down their tools and hurried home. The air was full of stories of mysticism and conspiracy. While the chroniclers mourned to have lost this gracious ruler who, though leaving the papacy unsullied, had let it descend into one of the least powerful forces in Europe, antagonistic parties slithered out from their holes like snakes.

"My heart is sore pained within me, and the terrors of death are fallen upon me," Cardinal Gonzales sighed, wiping a very large tear from his right eye. "Oh, it is so distressing. I was not there to catch him!"

"No need to fret," Di Quaglio smiled, putting his hand on the shaking shoulder of Gonzales. "Jesus said unto Simon, 'Fear not; from henceforth thou shalt catch men.'"

"Aye," O'Malley grinned. "But you have to be quick to catch them alive. At the present time we'd better be thinking about filling the office instead of whipping ourselves raw because an old fellow is enjoying a sweet bit of rest."

Dressed in the cardinalitial colours of red and black, like brightly wounded ravens, they swept in on the

Vatican City, important, each face encased in an austere mask, behind which swelled brains broiling with supramundane or mundane ambitions and plots. There were one hundred and seventeen of them, Cardinals, conclavists under the age of eighty, and each took up lodging in the Domus Sanctae Marthae, the accommodations being equivalent to those of any four-star hotel.

This group was particularly noteworthy for its large number of Latin Americans. Aside from Cardinal Gonzales from Mexico, who carried enormous weight, there was Cardinal Palafox from Argentina, Cardinal Velasco from Ecuador and Cardinal Núñez of Peru, as well as many others. It was thus widely expected that the next Pope would be from that part of the world, most likely in the person of one Cardinal Hernando Dominguez Hojeda, of Colombia, who the entire Latin American faction was backing.

The following morning the Cardinal electors gathered in the Basilica of Saint Peter and took part in the solemn Eucharistic celebration with the Votive Mass Pro Eligendo Papa. They then met for an early lunch of beef steak and rice before re-congregating in the Pauline Chapel of the Apostolic Palace, where they appeared in choir dress, invoked the assistance of the Holy Spirit with the chant of the Veni Creator, and then solemnly proceeded to the Sistine Chapel.

The conclave seated itself. The Cardinal Dean rose, cleared his throat and, in a voice swollen with importance, read: "We, the Cardinal electors present in this election of the Supreme Pontiff promise, pledge and swear to observe scrupulously the prescriptions contained in the Apostolic Constitution. We likewise promise, pledge and swear that whichever of us by divine disposition is elected Roman Pontiff will commit himself faithfully to carrying out the munus Petrinum of Pastor of the Universal Church and will not fail to affirm and defend strenuously the spiritual and temporal rights and the liberty of the Holy See. We promise and swear to observe with the greatest fidelity everything that in any way relates to the election of the Roman Pontiff and regarding what occurs in the place of the election, directly or indirectly related to the results of the voting, we promise and swear not to break this secret in any way, either during or after the election of the new Pontiff, unless explicit authorisation is granted by the same Pontiff; and never to lend support or favour to any interference, opposition or any other form of intervention, whereby secular authorities of whatever order and degree or any group of people or individuals might wish to intervene in the election of the Roman Pontiff."

Each Cardinal elector, placing his hand on the gospel, intoned: "This I do pledge and swear; so help me God and these Holy Gospels which I touch with my hand."

Four cardinals were nominated: Cardinal Hernando Dominguez Hojeda, of Colombia, Francois Villefort, of France, Mark Stewart of the United States, and Xaverio Torturo of Italy. Measures were taken, though surreptitiously, to verify the sex of the candidates. All were recognised as being admissible males.

The factions were clear and obvious:

It was known that Cardinal Villefort had once made a statement, albeit at a private gathering, that Italian food was poison. Though this is a not an uncommon opinion amongst the French, it was an opinion he would have been wiser to keep to himself. Cardinals, like schoolgirls, are prone to gossip. Villefort's words reached the ears of O'Malley, who made sure to bandy them about to his Italian brethren. There are three things which every Italian holds sacred: Their religion, their mother, and their pasta. Needless to say Villefort's culinary prejudice won him no points with the Italians. As they gathered for the conclave, there was not a one who did not swear they would be damned before they would place their vote with Villefort. Thanks to a number of behind the curtains meetings held by Zuccarelli, as well as a natural propensity to stand by their own, they were unanimously in favour of Torturo.

The American, Cardinal Stewart, was much heralded as the best candidate for "the Pope of the new millennium;" all the technological, financial and military advantages of his country being taken as the personal attributes of his character. The French particularly objected to Stewart on the grounds that his knowledge of scriptural matters was but rudimentary, the fellow not rightly understanding Latin liturgy, let alone Greek. The Germans and English, however, were all for the American, who they saw as one of their own. They defended him, saying that knowledge of Greek was hardly a requirement for the Supreme seat, taking the unfortunate example of Pope Alexander VI, who did not know a word of the language.

"Furthermore," Cardinal Hans Grünwald of Germany pointed out. "If we are going to be picky on these matters, let us not overlook the fact that the much respected South American candidate Cardinal Hojeda also does not have adept knowledge of the Greek tongue. It does not seem to me that a dead language should be a requirement for a living office."

As these arguments were being flung about, it naturally occurred that the qualifications of the fourth candidate, Cardinal Xaverio Torturo should be put under scrutiny. That he played a vital role in the reinstatement of the most holy relics of the holy saints was known by all, but, as he was somewhat of a newcomer to the cardinalature, his history was vague. When it became known that, not only could he speak Latin like Tacitus and Greek like the Archangel Gabriel, but knew the good book in either language by rote, many undecided members of the conclave could not help but murmur their approval. The French were hushed; the Germans could hardly object.

But, though the French had been bettered on matters of scholarship, the Americans, both South and North, had not been met with on the matter of spiritual qualifications.

Stewart was a stupid man who lived his life according to a more or less fundamentalist agenda. His stupidity was often hailed as saintly simplicity while his cringing sycophancy was easily labelled "moral fortitude." He had the utmost difficulty in stringing together ten words for a speech without making a gross blunder, but his round, childlike face and heinous accent lent him a naïveté that charmed as often as it repelled.

Cardinal Hojeda, in his own slick, oily way, smiled a great deal and often talked excitedly of poverty relief. His advocates took this as a spiritual stance, conveniently closing their eyes to the fact Hojeda was a two-faced liar who lived in a sumptuous fashion off the gifts of the cartel while large numbers of his people starved in unhygienic slums.

"Cardinal Hojeda is a man of the most pure heart," Gonzales said.

"There is no one more pious than Stewart," was Grünwald's blunt comment.

O'Malley, though part of the English faction, had a personal antipathy towards the North American candidate. He had met him once on a trip to New York, at an outdoor lawn party on Long Island. The two men were introduced. They shook hands and exchanged a few seemingly polite banalities. O'Malley, under the pretext of needing to get a glass of water, stepped behind a hedge to smoke a cigarette. However, while applying a match to a Lucky Strike, he overheard Stewart, stationed on the opposite side of the hedge, conversing with the third party who had introduced the two men. He made a few uncouth comments on O'Malley's appearance, and complained of an unpleasant odour which the Irishman emitted. As if that were not enough, the American proceeded to give a very unjust imitation of O'Malley's accent, a thing which the latter could hardly tolerate, particularly from an illiterate American. No man likes to hear that he smells and no man likes to be secretly mocked. Stewart was not only stupid, but it seemed that he was mean as well. It was no wonder that O'Malley did not want Cardinal Stewart to be the next Vicar of Christ upon Earth.

"Looking at the candidates put before us," O'Malley said, "I cannot help but feel that not enough has been said in favour of Cardinal Torturo. Now, though he is both younger and less known than either Hojeda or Stewart, it does not mean that he is any less a man of God. Youth means vigour; newness, a freshness of heart. If we peruse his history, a picture comes before us;—a picture of a man working quietly, devotedly in the service of our Lord. Amongst his colleagues at the Seminary it was well known that, not only did he spend his days in constant study of biblical matters, but he spent the hours of darkness in near unceasing prayer. His time was equally divided between the library and the chapel, while the dining hall saw him for but minutes at a time. The whole of his days and nights he consecrated to prayer and labour, devotion and industry. Does anyone challenge his priestly virtues? Can anyone claim that he be without prudence, justice, moral uprightness, loyalty, sobriety, faith, obedience, humility and piety? His youth was a diamond template which we would do well to have all our young men follow."

The cardinal, knowing well the art of oratory, paused. The Italians nodded their approval. The Latin Americans shifted uneasily in their seats. Licking his thin Irish lips O'Malley continued:

"This blessed Torturo it was who brought us back the tongue of Saint Anthony and the precious bones of our predecessors along this Catholic path of righteousness. We have, each one of us, heard whisperings of miracles and many here have seen with their own eyes things which they cannot explain away in mundane terms.—I speak of the tongue of Saint Anthony brought unscathed from flames.—Some of you might justly say that it was God who performed the miracle through the relic. Quite true: God performed the miracle through the relic using Cardinal Torturo, though then only a simple priest, as his conduit. Being a direct conduit to God, the Creator and Supreme Ruler of the Universe, is no small recommendation. I would go so far as to say it is the highest spiritual qualification. Cardinal Xaverio Torturo is certainly far more than just a superb scholar, he is a pious being without mitigation. Some have called for scholarship, others for more supramundane qualities.—Need a man know Greek for the office? We can suppose not, but it is obviously of advantage for one to comprehend the words of Saint Ignatius when he wrote, '*prokathemene tes agapes*,' since, after all, on such statements rest the entire validity of the Roman See. It seems obvious that we need a man who has not but one of these qualities, these qualities of Spirit and Intelligence, but a man whose cup runneth over with both.—Come, we each one of us know who that man is. In our heart of hearts we know. He has spent his life in obscurity, he has spent his life in poverty, he has spent his life in service to Our Lord. Let there be no mistake about it: This man, Xaverio Torturo, is the rightful successor of Saint Peter!"

The Cardinal Camerlengo called for the vote to be taken. The one hundred and seventeen cardinals all stared gravely before them, their backs to the brilliantly frescoed walls. The room was hot. Sweat rolled down from beneath their red caps. Ballot papers, on which were written "*Eligo in suumum pontificem*," were distributed. The cardinals each wrote their choice on a ballot and, one at a time approached the chalice, dropping the ballots within, kneeling and intoning, "I call to witness Christ the Lord who will be my judge, that my vote is given to the one who before God I consider should be elected."

The votes were counted by the Cardinal Camerlengo and his three assistants, or scrutineers. The first scrutineer read the name on each ballot aloud, wrote it down on a tally sheet and then passed the ballot to the next scrutineer who, in a steady voice that all could hear, confirmed the name and passed it to the third. The third, in his turn, recited the name chosen, then ran a needle and thread through the centre of each ballot, through the word "eligo," to join them all together. After all the ballots were read, the ends of the thread were tied and the ballots thus joined placed in an empty receptacle. The scrutineers then added up the totals for each candidate. Three revisers then double-checked the count.

Hojeda held his breath when the Camerlengo stood up to read the results. Villefort, who already had done a mental tally, scowled. Stewart and Torturo both looked unperturbed, the former from stupidity, the latter from fact.

Villefort received nineteen votes, Hojeda forty-three, Torturo thirty and Stewart twenty-five. Hojeda had the most votes. But, to be elected Pope, a candidate must receive more than two-thirds of the votes. Pope John Paul II made one slight variation to this rule, in order to free up deadlocks, which was to make it so that, if after thirty elections have taken place without any one Cardinal being elected Pope, then the Cardinals may elect by simple majority.—One thing was clear in the present match, however: Villefort and Stewart were out—the battle was between Hojeda and Torturo.

The Italians would have loved to see one of their own blood crown the glory of their country;—Unfortunately the conclave was made up of only seventeen percent Italians, the lowest number in history. Contrariwise, there were a full twenty-four percent Latin Americans, by far the highest in history.

After a tea break in which there was much excited whispering, a second vote was taken. All of Villefort's votes but one went to Hojeda, who also gained nine of Stewart's, giving him seventy. Torturo received forty-seven. Hojeda had the majority, but once again he lacked the two-thirds necessary to win.

That evening the Domus Sanctae Marthae was buzzing like a college dormitory. Cardinals floated from room to room, stating their opinions in meaningful undertones, exchanging gossip. Hojeda and Gonzales slithered through the halls, their faces beaming with confidence. Hojeda, who was making optimum use of his oily smile, only needed to secure eight more votes in order to be the next Pope. Like vultures the two men circled around Torturo's forty-seven, seeing which eight would be the easiest to pick away.

Meanwhile O'Malley, Zuccarelli and Di Quaglio spread out. O'Malley joked with the French cardinals, Di Quaglio whispered promises to the Germans and Americans, Zuccarelli threatened the South Americans and Africans.

The next day, when the conclave gathered in the Sistine Chapel, Gonzales winked at Hojeda, who responded by pursing his fat lips. Cardinal Velasquez from Spain saw this and found it distasteful. The vote was taken. Torturo received fifty-six votes and Hojeda sixty-one. Gonzales, upon hearing the outcome, grunted a few words of angry disappointment. O'Malley grinned with delight. Cardinal Velasquez, making his way out of the chapel, cut Gonzales.

During lunch, which consisted of fried fish and an artichoke salad, O'Malley, Zuccarelli and Di Quaglio worked the vote diligently. O'Malley charmed; Zuccarelli attempted to probe people's conscience.

Cardinal Núñez of Peru, when rising from table, became violently ill. His face was pale, he walked a few uncertain steps, and then fell to the floor, heaving miserably. He was given immediate medical attention, but to no avail, and thus had to be removed from the Vatican City and taken to the Salvator Mundi International Hospital in Rome. Though most blamed the fish, and a few the artichokes, some whispered that the poor Peruvian had been poisoned.

When the conclave reassembled in the Sistine Chapel and voted, Hojeda came off with fifty-nine and Torturo fifty-seven. Hojeda had lost two votes: one, most likely, had been Núñez, the other was a defector. Hojeda's position was visibly weakening.

The Camerlengo shrugged his shoulders and called for the vote to be taken again, for the third time that day. Hojeda had fifty-eight and Torturo had fifty-eight. Hojeda had lost yet another vote, bringing it to a dead draw. The next and fourth vote, however, showed unchanged results. Each man had an exactly equal portion of the votes.

From this point on there was no change. Each man held his ground. Though each party struggled, grappled to snatch away a vote or two from their opponents, the result was always the same: a deadlock. The conclave voted four times a day for six days until, in total, the conclave had voted thirty times. The next vote would be ruled by simple majority, yet each man still had an identical number of votes. Hojeda locked himself in his room and prayed, on his hands and knees, that Núñez would revive and re-enter the conclave, but report had it that the Peruvian was still extremely unwell—too sick to be moved.

O'Malley, Zuccarelli and Di Quaglio worked with manly vigour in an attempt to lure one of Hojeda's men over to their side, but Hojeda's fifty-seven (fifty-eight including Hojeda himself) were loyalists and inclined to rebuff the Italian faction with fluent contempt.

There was much tension in the air when the conclave assembled for the first vote which would be decided by simple majority. Gonzales looked bitterly at O'Malley while O'Malley murmured sarcastic remarks about Gonzales to his neighbour. Zuccarelli gave Hojeda a look of cold indifference while ingratiating himself as much as he could to the rest of Hojeda's faction, every man of which was in possession of that all precious deciding vote.

The Cardinal Camerlengo called for the vote to be taken. The ballot papers were being distributed when Torturo rose from his seat. "Cardinal Dean," he said, "do you mind if I make a quick comment to the assembly prior to the vote?"

"Such a proceeding is not usual, and only allowable for the most grave and urgent reasons."

"I fully realise this. What I desire to say is both grave and urgent, as it reflects on the whole validity of the process we are about to perform."

There was a murmur amongst the assembly.

"Then it cannot wait to be said until after the vote?"

"No."

"In that case, we have no choice I suppose. Speak, but be brief."

"Thank you, Cardinal Dean, I shall," Torturo said, prowling out into the centre of the great hall. His gaze swept over the faces before him, settling on Cardinal Gonzales. "Cardinal," he said. "We have now been at the assembly for nine days, correct?"

"That is correct," Gonzales answered curtly, obviously annoyed.

"What is the date today?"

"April the third, I believe."

"Believe indeed! You are absolutely correct." Torturo smiled and stepped closer to the old man. "A very special day, is it not?"

"Considering it is the day we are likely to elect the Successor to Saint Peter, it certainly is, a most blessed day."

"But for no other reason?"

Gonzales did not reply.

"Come, sir. Is there no other reason?"

"Cardinal Torturo!" The Cardinal Camerlengo objected in a raised voice. "I certainly hope you have good reason for this line of questioning—this browbeating. Can you not see that you are aggravating the good cardinal?"

"I can."

"Then what is your purpose; why do you proceed?"

"Because of the day Cardinal Dean;—Because of the day."

"And what has the day anything to do with it?"

"It has everything to do with it when the day is April the third of the year ****."

"Enlighten the assembly."

"It has everything to do with it when the day is April the third of the year **** and the good Cardinal Gonzales was born on the April the third of the year ****."

There was a moment of silence followed by murmurs of extreme agitation. Gonzales cringed.

"Yes," Torturo continued ruthlessly, "the day has everything to do with it when it is the good Cardinal's birthday, his eightieth birthday. He looks well for his age, does he not? Unfortunately, that is of no moment. The rules are quite specific: Only cardinals *under* eighty years of age are allowed to vote.—Sir," (turning to Gonzales). "Sir, on behalf of the congregation I jointly wish you a happy birthday and request that you depart before the voting begins.—By law your vote can no longer be counted."

Gonzales was flabbergasted. Many were mortified. The congregation was in an uproar. Cardinals, some with faces red with rage, others, all blood drained from their startled features, gestured and argued in uncontrolled agitation.

"Silence!" the Cardinal Dean demanded, in a raised voice. "Is this true," he asked when relative calm had been restored. "Is this true Gonzales? Is today really your eightieth birthday?"

"I . . . I don't rightly know," the cardinal said with embarrassment. "I . . . I suppose it is—It had—It had slipped my mind, but . . . But I do believe it is."

Hojeda rose to his feet. "What time were you born?" he demanded abruptly, looking at his watch. "It is now 10:30 a.m.; what time were you born?"

"I . . . I can't exactly recollect."

"It was in the afternoon probably. Was it not in the afternoon? You would not be eighty yet if it was in the afternoon."

"Yes, possibly," Gonzales mumbled. "It might have been in the afternoon."

"No need to worry on that score," Torturo said coolly, reaching in his pocket and producing a sheaf of papers. "I took the liberty of acquiring his birth certificate as well as affidavits from both his cousin and sister. The cousin is ten years older than the cardinal and his sister seven years older. Both distinctly remember the time of his birth as being in the early morning, which the birth certificate reaffirms, stating the hour to have been 2:45 a.m. He was born in Manizales, Columbia where, at this moment, it is 3:30 a.m. There can be no question about it: The man before us, though yesterday only seventy-nine years of age and eligible to vote, is today eighty and not in the least eligible for such a privilege."

Gonzales, white as a ghost, rose to his feet. He looked appealingly at the Cardinal Camerlengo, and then at Hojeda. The former shook his head solemnly, the latter bared his teeth. Gonzales shuffled out of the room, muttering a few muddled words as he went, which no one cared to hear and no one heard.

The vote was taken, and then counted by the Cardinal Camerlengo and his three assistants. The revisers double-checked the count and then the Camerlengo stood up and read the results. Out of the hundred and fifteen votes, there were fifty-seven for Hojeda and fifty-eight for Torturo.

The master of ceremonies, not paying attention to the instructions given by the custodian concerning the appropriate chemicals to be added when burning the ballots, ended up giving puzzling indications to the people assembled in St. Peter's Square. A plume of white smoke would indicate that a new Pope had been elected, while black would signal that a decision had not yet been reached. The smoke was dark grey. The people in St. Peter's Square murmured in confusion. Many insisted that the smoke was black, and that there was not yet a new Pope, while others were adamant in their belief that the smoke they had seen was white. The old men wagged their heads knowingly. The media debated the issue over ten thousand broadcasts.

Meanwhile, the one hundred and fifteen Cardinals adjourned from the Sistine Chapel to the Throne Room.

O'Malley took hold of Torturo's elbow as they entered. "We've done it, lad," he whispered in a cheerful voice.

Torturo smiled slightly, nodded, took a pack of Parisiennes from his pocket and lit one.

The cardinals assembled on both sides of the room, with the Cardinal Camerlengo poised in the middle, before the throne. Exhaling a plume of smoke, Torturo approached.

The Cardinal Camerlengo intoned:

"The Sacred College has elected Your Holy Excellence as the Bishop of Rome, Archbishop of the Roman Province, Primate of Italy, Summus Pontifex, Pontifex Maximus, Successor of Saint Peter, thereby the Chief Pastor of the Entire Church, Single Patriarch of the Entire Western Church, the Universal Church, the Vicar of Christ Upon Earth; the said position being yours and yours alone provided you are willing to take the office. Do you accept your canonical election as Supreme Pontiff?"

There was a pause.

Zuccarelli held his breath. He could hear his own heart throbbing in his chest. He looked at O'Malley. O'Malley bit his bottom lip and locked his twinkling eyes on the candidate. The entire room was frozen in anticipation.

Torturo took a puff of his cigarette.

"Certainly I am willing to take the office," he said, flicking away the half-smoked cylinder. "Let us indulge in the papacy since God has given it to us."

A sigh of relief and amazement swept across the room like a putrid Venetian breeze. O'Malley winked at Zuccarelli, giving him the thumbs up. Zuccarelli, for possibly the third or fourth time in his life, smiled a genuine smile. Cardinals nodded; double chins undulated. A vast number of handkerchiefs were applied to sweat-glistened foreheads. The room was monstrously hot.

Silence was called for. The Cardinal Camerlengo looked appropriately grave.

Gazing steadfastly at Torturo he asked: "By what name do you wish to be called?"

"Lando the Second."

Three-quarters of an hour later Torturo stood dressed in pontifical white. He received the triple crown unmoved, without the slightest sign of either elation or contempt. The cardinals, one by one, advanced towards Lando the Second and swore their submission.

The Dean of the College of Cardinals stepped out onto the balcony of the Vatican Basilica. The people stared up from below. The wind could be heard beating against his vestments, which flapped like the flag of a conquering army. He cupped his hands around his mouth, like a horn. "Habemus Papam!" he yelled. "We have a Pope!"

There was a roar of excitement. Fists of approbation were raised in the air. A sprightly old man began to dance in the court. Broad smiles flashed like jewels. Pope Lando the Second advanced out onto the balcony. The ovation he received was tremendous. The Italian people considered it a supreme victory. The noise of the

133

cheers could be heard throughout the city; they echoed against the hills and soared through the air like mighty birds. The Pope raised his hands and the people were hushed. All eyes were raised in joyful, serious attention. In a voice of absolute and unquestionable authority he pronounced the Apostolic Blessing Urbi et Orbi, and then returned within.

Two days later the coronation procession took place. A trumpet sounded. Rome fell silent. The Pope stepped outside, a white, almost phallic streak that moved with awesome gravity down the steps of St. Peter's Basilica, onto the square. He carried in one hand, like a staff, the erect cross. The crowd parted, as if cloven in two by an axe. Two women fainted. The heels of his shoes could be heard on the brickwork. A magnificent white boulonnais horse was brought forth, which he mounted. He made his way down the via della Conciliazione and then along the Corso Vittorio Emanuele II. Nine hundred priests and cardinals followed him. There were floats displaying allegorical images and draped with pithy Latin sayings. Many fell to their knees as he passed. All remarked on the dignity of the new Pope's appearance.

During those first days and nights the Roman people celebrated the ordination of the new Pope as if it were Carnival. The revel and rejoicing was enthusiastic to an unparalleled degree. It was like a massive, unmitigated public orgy. There were bonfires in the streets, songs sung and candlelight processions. Pictures of Torturo, now Lando the Second, hung from windows and were stationed around the city's great monuments amongst garlands of flowers. All shops were closed and, young and old alike, paraded through the streets in uninterrupted merriment. The Pope was vernal; the Pope was Italian. Wine and bread were given out gratis. Barilla made a special pasta, in the shape of a fish, and dubbed it landotori for the occasion. Even some Protestants were pleased with the choice; the city of Bern struck off a medal in his honour.

Others, those Christians more radically opposed to popishness, declaimed him as the Antichrist.

XIII

THE day after his coronation the new pope called Vivan and Zuccarelli to him, for a private audience.

The two men were shown through the Sala degli Arazzi, its walls adorned with magnificent Gobelin tapestries, into the Throne Room. Pope Lando the Second sat at the far end, on his majestic seat. He was dressed all in white, except for a crimson hood which sat on his shoulders. A priceless Spanish carpet lay between the door and the throne. Vivan stepped forward first, minced through the stately chamber, climbed the steps leading to the throne and fell to his knees, kissing the Pope's right foot, which rested on a crimson pillow. Zuccarelli strode forward. Five metres before the Pope he dropped to one knee, bowed and rose. He proceeded forward, climbed the steps to the throne, bowed and kissed the Pope's hand.

Pope Lando the Second spoke.

"Both of you have been of inestimable service," he said gravely, "and, now that I am in a position to show my appreciation, I intend to do so."

Zuccarelli nodded his head, as if to say: "I expected nothing less."

"The three of us have a bond," the Pope continued. "Though not strictly a bond of friendship, it is none the less precious. Though it is true that spirituality and perfection are not necessarily connected with advancement in our holy order, we still, each of us, are happy to advance. I have advanced. You shall each advance. We advance together."

Vivan was affected. His eyes became watery. He was speechless.

The Primate of Italy proceeded:

"Cardinal Zuccarelli, I bestow on you the post of Secretary of State of the Vatican and also make you Cardinal-Deacon with the title of SS. Silvestro e Martino ai Monti."

Zuccarelli bowed. "I am honoured," he said.

"Bishop Vivan, I make you my personal assistant in all matters, as well as Cardinal-Priest with the title SS. Cosmas e Damian."

"Oh, wonderful!" Vivan giggled and then, after giving a great, sweeping bow, fell to his knees and kissed the Pope's hand. "Did I not tell you his offer was good?" he said, rising and turning to Zuccarelli.

Zuccarelli admitted it was so.

"Oh, we have wonderful days ahead of us," Vivan cried, clapping his palms together. "And my mother will be thrilled—simply thrilled!"

"We are certainly in an enviable position," Zuccarelli commented.

"Your positions *certainly are* enviable," the Pope said, "and I feel confident that your time will be spent both agreeably and productively. That is as it should be. But I do have one condition to impose."

Both men looked up inquiringly. Zuccarelli stuck out his chin.

"My only condition to bestowing these titles, to sharing all this opulence with the two of you, is that you both do me credit. Use the salt of prudence. Make sure not to dishonour me. Do not sully your offices. Be discreet."

"Discreet, Holy Father?" Vivan asked.

"Yes. You probably have not run across the word yet in your reading, but I expect you to learn its definition: I require you to be both careful and tactful in what you say and do."

"I am sure you will find no reason to complain of our behaviour or regret your trust," Zuccarelli said.

"I do not suppose it otherwise. I am simply stating the obvious so that there is no mistake. Now: Later in the week we will meet in order to outline your exact duties. Meanwhile I imagine you each have many things to wrap up back in Padua. Please do so and return as quickly as possible: Your residences from henceforth are here, in the Vatican, near my person."

Both men expressed their complete compliance, bowed and moved towards the exit. Vivan turned, on his way out, and blinked.

"Is there anything else?" the Primate of Italy asked.

"Oh, nothing," Vivan blushed. "I only wanted to say that you look exceptionally *majestic* in white!"

The door shut behind the two ecclesiastics. The Pope rose from his seat and began to pace the room. His dormant season was at an end. It was now the time for action; he needn't hide his light under a bushel. The world expected great things from him, and he had every determination to give the world great things.

He sent a message to Di Quaglio, requesting his immediate presence. Ten minutes later the plump little man came bustling into the Throne Room, a giant leather ledger under one arm. He bowed.

"You wanted to see me *Summus Pontifex*?"

"Yes. There are a few matters I want to discuss with you. In the time of my predecessor, you were the Secretary of Finance of the Vatican, were you not?"

"I was."

"That will not do."

"Oh!"

"That will not do. I want you nearer to my person."

"As you wish Holy Father."

"You were a great help during the conclave, and I believe you are fit for greater responsibilities. Would you object to being the Sub-Prefect of the Sacred Apostolic Palace?"

"Not in the least, Your Holiness!"

"You will retain your original position as Secretary of Finance, but you will have this one as well,—But you must pledge to me your complete subservience and obedience."

"I—I do," the little man stammered.

"You must keep an eye out for my interests. Watch over all my underlings. Report to me any mischief you discover."

"Certainly."

"Monitor all comings and goings."

"Certainly."

"Monitor the phone lines."

"Yes, *Summus Pontifex*."

"What is that you have under your arm?"

"The ledger summing up the finances of the Vatican."

"Fine, set it down over there . . . Yes, that will do."

"Do you require me further?"

"Yes;—I have business to conduct . . . I want all public access cut off from the Sistine Chapel and the Vatican museums."

"But, Your Holiness, to deny public access . . ."

"Yes, deny it. The residential section around the Cortile de San Domasco is ridiculously small for the sole Patriarch of the Western Church. Of the thousand or so rooms, only two hundred are set aside for my use, a quantity which is grossly inadequate. The chapel as well as the majority of museum buildings must be sequestered for private purposes."

"Your Holiness, I am not sure if you realise it or not, but the chapel, aside from being a most sanctified place, is also a considerable source of capital. Millions of tourists visit it each year and, at nine euros a head . . ."

"My dear fellow," the Pope said imperiously, "I am not a cattle rancher or pig farmer to be concerned with head-count, nor do I much fancy my residence as a kind of Catholic Disney Land. It would be greatly appreciated if you did not second guess my decisions. Remember, Christ proclaimed that it was my choice to bind or loose as I choose. The legislative authority of Saint Peter falls upon me . . . The relics of the holy saints will, in any case, remain in Rome. If people want to pay to see something, let it be those, and let them be enlightened thereby. The most important task for you at present is to make sure that the holy personage who utters these words is scrupulously obeyed and comforted. Going against the grain, the grain being I, is not a habit of which the cultivation is recommended."

Just as Pius II, Paul II and Innocent VIII made changes to the Papal residence, so did the present *Summus Pontifex*. Pope Lando the Second cared not a whit what the world might think. His fists were made not to coddle but to crush. The Vatican, partially cleared of its touristic and pecuniary aspect, was thus greatly increased in useable size.

Leonardo's *St. Jerome* and the *Stefaneschi* triptych of Giotto he had removed to his own sleeping chambers. The paintings which defaced the walls of the modern picture gallery were removed and, along with the giant canvas by Matejko, sold at auction. The entire collection of Egyptian antiquities, except for the papyri, he had returned to the government of that country, a move which gained him much acclaim in previously antagonistic quarters.

Vivan, instructed to decorate his chambers as he pleased and given full access to the Vatican treasures of art, exposed his feral nature. Being an adamant admirer of manly beauty, he placed, in the centre of his office, the giant gilt bronze statue of Hercules which Pius IX had paid such vast sums for. Around this he stationed the Apollo Sauroktonos, a bust of a young boy from the Sala dei Busti, and the Satyr from the Gabinetto delle Maschere. The walls he hung with valuable tapestries and paintings, including some by Guido Reni, Titian and Caravaggio. Small Greek sculptures, from the Galleria Chiaramonti, he scattered throughout the corners and nooks, paying no heed to which were originals and which reproductions, and interspersed them with Etruscan vases. His cabinets he filled with vessels of all type and shape, including a kylix by Xenophantos, an amphora by Epiktetos and a somewhat risque majolica plate by Georgio Andreoli. Next to his desk he placed the Belvedere Apollo.

The wonderful Sistine Chapel, one hundred and thirty-three feet long and forty-six feet wide, cleared of the ever-stampeding train of upright livestock, was quickly converted into an office for Pope Lando the Second, where he could comfortably go about the business of the day in an environment that was to his liking. The tasteless, manneristic end frescoes over the door he had replaced by a Roman mosaic of the third century with figures of a stag and birds and another mosaic taken from the Porto San Lorenzo depicting Achilles dragging the body of Hector. A large oak desk was set up beneath *The Last Judgment*, upon which he put his writing gear and a telephone that was connected to the outer office where his secretary, Cardinal-Priest Vivan, sat, admiring the Belvedere torso while awaiting instructions.

"It is most unusual," Cardinal Gonzales complained when he saw the alterations taking place. "After all, this is the court chapel and is considered to be reserved for papal ceremonies and elections. Thus, even if we are to deny public access, I am not sure if it is acceptable for use as an office."

"Signore Gonzales, my using the chapel as an office will in no way impede the usual ceremonies," was the reply of the Archbishop of the Roman Province. "I am flexible. The ceremonies which previously took place here will be transposed to the Cappella Paolina. As for your second point: A papal election can only take place when I am dead. Under such circumstances I would certainly not object to your doing as you wish with the space."

The sole Patriarch of the Western Church naturally had his way. This chamber, the famous Sistine Chapel, was, for the most part, kept sparse. The frescoes of Michelangelo, Perugino, Pinturicchio, Botticelli, Ghirlandajo, Pier di Cosimo, Rosselli, Signorelli and della Gatta were the sole décor on the walls. The twelve stained-glass windows, which had been given by the Prince Regent Leopold of Bavaria, were removed, sold at auction by Sotheby's and replaced by plain semi-opaque glass, which let in far more light and were not half so ugly. Toward the back end of the room, the last third beyond the beautiful marble barrier, His Holiness set up a personal library of those books and manuscripts which he felt a need of immediate access to. In the centre, more or less beneath the *Creation of Adam*, was a small wooden table, big enough to seat four, on which were perpetually placed equipment for satisfying his hunger at any hour, *videlicet*, a jug of Montepulciano

143

wine, a partial form of parmigiano reggiano, a bowl of black olives and a loaf of rye bread. A young man from Mantova named Lucio was kept in an outer chamber, stationed before an espresso machine, his sole job being to make the said beverage at an instant's notice, at any given hour of the day or night, and have it delivered within two minutes of its being asked for at the door of the potentate.

He had a couch set up to one side of the room upon which to lie and at the far end he kept glass cases containing items particular to himself: the skin of a bush-cat, eagles' claws, snail shells, feathers, tails and heads of snakes, the horns of antelopes, goats and gazelles, a dried buffalo's liver, the teeth and claws of a leopard, herbs and nuts. He had no intention whatsoever of neglecting his studies. Though he was far from a fool, he was not devoid of pride. He had had great successes and believed himself capable of still greater. Christ Jesus had been sent forth from the presence of the invisible beings as a saviour, for the deliverance of men. Lando would also deliver men;—deliver them from their own wickedness, and let it be seen that he too was a saviour. From the abyss of darkness he would rule with the light of justice and truth. He was convinced that his mission was not far from divine.

He brought his cousin Marco from Padua and had him ordained, something the poor man had long wished for. Marco shed tears of joy. His heart danced in his chest.

"Thank you ever so much, Holy Father," he said. "I am extremely eager to begin my religious duties."

"Certainly," the Pope replied, "but please be aware that I might call on you if I need help with security measures."

"Security measures?"

"Yes. If I need to implement disciplinary measures I might call on you. Be prepared."

Meanwhile Gonzales was finding his position in the Vatican more and more untenable. During the previous Pope's reign he had been of supreme importance, influencing the feeble old man in almost all decisions of moment. With Lando it was different. Not only had he gravely embarrassed Gonzales during the conclave, but now that he was in office, he had stripped him of nearly all his responsibilities. Gonzales spent his days wandering about the palace like a ghost, seeing activity everywhere but unable to take a meaningful role in any of it. Even the majority of South American cardinals, following the dictates of self-interest, had more or less abandoned him.

"What do you expect?" Hojeda said. "You failed to get me elected and now, in my place, we have an Italian who tells us to quit our missionary exploits along the Amazon Basin. He seems to think that the indigenous people are not in need of salvation."

"A man like this cannot last long," Gonzales said.

"Not last long? He is not yet forty years old and he seems to be in optimum health. I believe he will see us both in our graves."

"No," Gonzales insisted desperately. "He cannot last long."

Cardinal Gonzales, though by no means a brilliant man, could not help but see that the new Pope desired to change the course of the Catholic church. He missed no opportunity to whisper calumnies against the successor of Saint Peter. "It is a frightening thing," he would say, "when we consider the vision of the angel Gabriel, and how he describes a king of a most fierce countenance who understands dark questions, and is exceedingly powerful, and full of false wonders. Gabriel says that he shall corrupt, direct, influence, and put strong and holy men down. He will derail the Church. Deceit shall be in his hand, and he will lead many to perdition, bruising them in his hand like eggs."

The Pope meanwhile worked with activity. He did indeed desire to change the course of the Church and took no pains to hide the fact. It seemed to him a crude thing to spend so much effort in the proselytization of third world nations. The men who were assigned such tasks were usually brutes of feeble intellect who no more understood the words of the gospel than parrots. To have such men as his representatives he considered to be disgraceful. As it was, the faith of Europeans was in the midst of a remarkable decline. There was an upsurge in young Italian atheists. The priesthood was in a state of decay. For the most part, only the most feeble young men, young men who were too weak to endure the hardships of the real world, took up the calling.

"Our duty lies pre-imminently in our homeland," he said. "We need to make Christ Jesus fashionable once more. We need to divert our youth from the football field and into the seminary. We must herd our young women out of the discotheques and into the nunneries."

"But young people these days want to join the workforce," Di Quaglio suggested. "They wish to be part of the world economy."

"World economy be damned!" the sole Patriarch of the Western Church cried in annoyance. "Italy is the greatest nation on earth and I will see it burning in hell before I see it turned into the slave of Brussels. The nation that produced Leonardo da Vinci, Dante and Machiavelli will not be the producer of light bulbs and eyeglasses for England and America."

XIV

CARDINALS, when given an audience with him, quivered from head to toe. Those used to addressing assemblies of thousands found themselves speechless in his singular presence. The President of the United States, upon visiting Rome for the first time, obtained an audience for himself, his wife and daughter. The latter two dressed themselves in black, with black veils, like women from Sicily. The daughter wore red shoes, grotesquely incongruous with the occasion.

"Red shoes!" Di Quaglio whispered to the Pope as they approached.

"A dash of the Scarlet Woman in her, eh?"

For the Vicar of Christ Upon Earth, the meeting was tiresome. The presence of the women, the nature of the visit, made the discussion of serious topics difficult to advance. He was glad to leave the Throne Room at the end of such a dull audience. He made his way through the Gallery of Maps, the walls rich with rare charts, cosmographical diagrams and paintings of naval battles. Turning the corner, into the Sala Dei Misteri, he saw Zuccarelli moving towards him with hasty steps, his face solemn and particularly dignified. Since his ascension to the important office he now held, the tall, thin ecclesiastic seemed more grave and distinguished than ever. Though he treated the Pope with the utmost respect, those of lesser status he glanced over with a level of contempt that made him notorious.

"Good day," Lando the Second said, offering the other his hand.

Zuccarelli quickly dropped to one knee, kissed the Pope's hand and rose. "Good day, Your Holiness."

"And how are you?"

"Perfect."

"Are you finding your new situation satisfactory?"

"Yes, absolutely satisfactory," Zuccarelli answered stiffly. "Most kind of you to ask."

"I take it that you are having no trouble in managing the affairs of the various departments under your jurisdiction? The departments of building, furnishing, and household expenses I imagine to be of little trouble, aside from the accounting. And the fire brigade, garage, printing presses and gardening department, being self-contained in nature, must more or less run themselves."

"Well, they do not exactly run themselves, but Di Quaglio, in his role of sub-prefect, takes a certain portion of the workload off my shoulders, so in the end things are manageable."

"Di Quaglio is a good man."

"He knows his work."

"And Vivan, have you seen him? I would like to consult with him about certain matters."

"I believe he is in the Sala degli Arazzi, taking lunch. I saw him and a few—I saw him and a few friends making their way there earlier, and was told something to that effect."

"The Sala degli Arazzi? I did not realise it was a dining room. But, following your suggestion, I will look for him there. And you? You seem to be in a hurry. Does duty call?"

"Er. Yes; duty does call. A number of important tasks . . ."

The Pope nodded his head. "I would imagine so," he said. "Your responsibilities are extensive."

Zuccarelli muttered a few unintelligible words, presumably an adieu, bowed, turned and, resuming his hasty steps, made his way around the corner, towards his own private chambers.

After watching the cardinal retreat, the Pope resumed his own course, his face grown more austere since the encounter. The Swiss Guards along the way stood like statues, the blood draining from their faces as the Primate of Italy passed them by. What persons he met fell hushed to their knees in his presence, like poppies before Tarquin, not daring to so much as lift their eyes beyond the level of his knees.

At the great carved double doors of the Sala degli Arazzi the Primate of Italy stopped. He could hear voices coming from within and a great deal of laughter;—the giggling of Vivan was particularly pronounced.

The Pope pushed one door open and stepped silently into the room. In the centre was a table, surrounded by young men, with Vivan at its head. The walls of the room, decorated with colourful landscape frescoes worked around the arms of Paul V, beneath which hung valuable Flemish tapestries, were beautifully imposing. The ceiling was thoroughly gilt. The windows, high and stately, were covered with white silk, backed by the same material in green. The marble floor was a priceless work of art in itself, with elaborate scenes depicted in the most ornate mosaic.

The Pope silently observed the young men who surrounded the table. Each was distinctly handsome in the way that models are: that is, merely physically attractive with eyes gleaming simplicity rather than emotional or intellectual depth. The eight or so youths were each dressed in various costumes of green fabric and leather, clothes truly designed for the catwalk rather than public usage. One had on an enormous hat like that in Pisanello's painting of Saint George in the London National Gallery, locks of his black hair curling out over his forehead. Another wore an ermine cape died a light, lime green. A third was attired from head to toe in granny Smith coloured snakeskin: a one-button jacket and close-fitting trousers that terminated at the ankle. The suit was obviously the production of one of the better Italian designers and must have carried a shocking price tag.

Vivan himself was dressed in a jumpsuit, very much in the cut of a mechanic's. Of course mechanics rarely have their garments hued to a rich bottle-green, and never tailored of sumptuous Japanese silk, much less adorned with a fish scale pattern and hung with leather tassels around the shoulders.

151

The Bishop of Rome coughed and walked forward, his heels clicking on the floor.

"Ah, hello most Holy Father," Vivan said, rising from his seat and waving his hand. "Won't you come and join us at our supper? These are some friends of mine,—Genuine Roman youths: Filippo, Alberto, Walter, Francesco, Vittorio, Franco, Dario and Terisio. See," (laughing), "I remember all their names!"

The eight youths stood up when they saw the Pope walk in. They were shy. They bowed. Dario, the boy with the snakeskin suit, blushed to the roots of his hair.

"What is this?" the Bishop of Rome asked, striding forward. "All dressed in green?"

"Yes," Vivan cried in a high-pitched voice. "Isn't it a jolly idea? Yesterday we had lavender day and today we are having green day! Tomorrow I wanted to have blue day, but Walter said he looks terrible in blue, so we might do pink instead."

The boy with the cape on looked down and bit his bottom lip. It was obviously Walter.

"Yes, blue does not suit redheads," the Pope said.

Walter opened his mouth. His lips trembled. "Thank you, Your Holiness," he whispered, not daring to raise his eyes.

"And what have we here?" Lando the Second took in the table at a glance.

Vivan giggled. "As I said, it's green day, so everything is green—not only the boys and I, but the food too! See," (extending a finger towards the various dishes), "we have green oysters, asparagus soup, crayfish swimming in lime sauce, rabbit with spinach, artichokes, ostrich in capers, and a lovely tossed salad."

"And this one?" the Pope asked, pointing to a magnificent sea-green majolica bowl by Flaminio Fontane, which he recognised as belonging to the Vatican treasury. The bowl was nearly brim-full of a dark grey slop, the odour of which distinctly reached his nose from where he stood, a metre away.

"Oh, yes, I cheated on our little colour rule for Dario's sake. This dish has become his favourite: mullet's viscera with black truffles. He is absurdly fond of truffles. Would you like to try it? I am sure the lad wouldn't mind."

The Pope, on the plea of having recently eaten, excused himself. He was far from trusting the effects of gormandising, knowing that it was salubrious to neither body nor mind. Rich foods, he believed, made one both weak and stupid. He asked Vivan for a moment of private intercourse. The two men walked to one side of the room, to the enclosure of a window, where their words could not be overheard.

"What is on your mind?" Vivan smiled. "You look very serious this afternoon. Did you get another one of those unpleasant letters from the Prime Minister of China?"

The successor of Saint Peter did not answer.

"You have been busy?" he asked.

"Oh, yes! So nonsensically busy! Busier than ever in my life I think. The amount of social intercourse I engage in is simply astounding!"

"Yes, you seem to be profiting well by the legend of Christ," the Pope said with quiet gravity.

Vivan cocked his head and raised his eyebrows.

"Excuse me?" he said. He either did not understand or did not choose to understand.

"It is obvious that you have not disdained the luxury that your position allows you access to," the Pope continued. "I can possibly tolerate this. But a few trivial tasks I asked you to perform have been neglected."

"Neglected?" Vivan blushed.

"Yes. My *Treatise on the Precious Blood* which I asked you, two days ago, to send to the translators so that it could be rendered into English, Japanese and German: I saw it on your desk this morning, apparently neglected. Last week I asked you to see that sixty thousand euros were wired to Cardinal Emmanuel Shiv in India for relief of the poor. He called me, not two hours ago, saying that the money has not yet been received."

Vivan turned towards the window. It was covered with silk and he could not see without.

"I must have forgotten. I will attend to it."

"Please do."

Presently the doors opened at the far end of the room. The Pope and Vivan both looked over. A man and a woman walked in, the former holding an acoustic guitar, the latter a tambourine.

"I will leave you now," the Pope said.

"Oh, but the musicians are just arriving!" Vivan cried gleefully. "Won't you stay and enjoy the show? Today we have 'folk' music from America."

The musicians had seated themselves on chairs off to one side of the room. The man was tuning his guitar. The woman stared brazenly at the Pope, one hand pushing her oily blonde hair away from her eyes.

"So you will stay?" Vivan asked again, gently rubbing the Pope's elbow.

"No, thank you," the other replied, pulling away. "Unfortunately my time is not my own. Unfortunately as *Servus servorum Dei*, as the Servant of the Servants of God, my time is not my own."

The Pope took his leave, nodding to the young men and walking out with brisk steps. The sound of the guitar and the twangy female voice of the American woman followed him out of the room.

"*How many roads must a man walk down,*" the singing went.

XV

POPE LANDO THE SECOND stood atop the Monumento a Vittorio Emanuele II, looking over the city of Rome stretched before him. The monument was majestic, pompous, just like the man it was dedicated to. The charioteers seemed more symbolic of the King of Piedmonte's moustache than anything else; the colossal cavalier, in the very centre of the monument, an abstraction of his goatee. The sun was set and the Pope was disguised in a shabby wool suit and red wig. He had needed exercise and freedom of movement and had snuck out of the Vatican thus disguised. These secret tactics had become a habit of his; he treasured these incognito hours when his mind flowed smoothly and his most ingenious thoughts were born.

"This city is mine," he thought to himself as he gazed over the vast surface of antique houses, bits of old ruin and glorious palazzos.

Feeling a sense of supreme dominance within him as his eyes met the dome of St. Peter's rising in the distance, he ejected a cigarette from his pack and lit it, breathing in the ill but flavourful smoke with joy.

He stalked down the steps to his right, past the Palazzo Nuovo and onto the Piazza del Campidoglio, the beautiful square designed by Michelangelo which sits like a nest atop Rome. A woman in flowing but tasteless wedding garments and a man, stiff in a rented tuxedo, were poised by the fountain, smiling into a half dozen cameras which snapped away at them. A rather dubious looking individual, dressed in blue sweatpants, a green shirt, a fishing cap and thick-rimmed glasses stood near the grand steps, the Cordonata. Lando gazed at the newlyweds. They displayed two sickeningly sweet smiles. He turned his eyes towards the steps. The man in the fishing cap showed him his back and proceeded to urinate against the base of one of the mighty statues which stood at either end of the steps.

"*Basta*!" the Pope murmured to himself as he escaped, towards the Temple of Jove. "Humans are a perverse species and certainly only a few of us deserve to have power in our hands."

Whether he deserved his position or not, Lando the Second, both young and intelligent, did seem exceptionally capable of handling the burden of power. He had a remarkable capacity for work and, in a short period, had managed to get much accomplished. He had rearranged matters of the treasury and, in order to curtail expenses, reduced the Vatican staff by ten percent. Energetically he suppressed unnecessary offices and enacted rigorous penalties for the misappropriation of church funds. He patronised learning, establishing chairs of Arabic, Hebrew and Syriac at all Catholic universities and founding a school of ancient Greek in Jakarta where he proposed to maintain a thousand students at his own expense.

His reputation as a man of wonders grew daily. The miracles he had performed at Padua were on every tongue and the incidents that had occurred since his coronation served well to add fuel to the fire of fanaticism. Lando did have to smile when he thought of all the freaks that found him. While delivering a discourse the previous week in Orvieto, half a dozen farmers had made their way into the church with a hog. The creature, of enormous proportions, tusked and rippling with pink fat, was bound with heavy ropes and it was all the men could do to keep it from bursting forth and running rampant through the congregation. The hog's eyes were bloodshot, its mouth foamed and its swollen tongue hung all the way to the floor. It snorted and howled hideously. The farmers stated that the pig had killed all the others in the herd and was possessed by a devil. The Pope stepped down from the pulpit and told them to release it. They did so with hesitation and then fled, as did the greater part of the congregation.

"You do not alarm me, devil," the Pope informed the sow in Latin. He stretched forth his hand. "Huge though your present body be; whether you inhabit a fox or a camel, you are just the same."

The brute, raging and looking as if it would devour Lando, approached, sheets of thick, white saliva hanging from its jaws. It pawed the ground, as if preparing for attack, but instead immediately collapsed, laying its head on the ground. To the amazement of all present, the swine suddenly exhibited as much tameness as it had ferocity before.

Di Quaglio was forced to send away delegations of sick on a daily basis. The Pope simply did not have time to lay hands on every cripple that walked through the doors of St. Peter's. These sick, however, were not to be put off. They would wait until Lando was to make a public appearance and then way-lay him, thrusting before him their grievances and ills.

"It is most troublesome," Di Quaglio commented. "Your Holiness is getting something of a reputation as a faith healer."

"And why is that troublesome, if it raises confidence in the power of God?"

"Well—because many say it is not respectable."

"My dear Di Quaglio; I am not a banker or politician, but the Pope; what do I care for people's respect!"

The truth was that the churches of Rome had never been fuller. The new Pope seemed to be re-popularising Christianity. His grave, handsome face attracted women and his athletic figure and manly bearing gained the respect of men. He was both a scholar and an able administrator who was considered to deserve not only praise but also the highest veneration.

The Vicar of Christ Upon Earth bent over and pressed the palms of his hands to the floor. Gradually he let the full weight of his body translate to the palms, while bending his elbows and resting his knees upon them. He nestled into the "crow" posture, stayed thus a quarter of an hour and then slowly rose into a handstand.

He stood in this manner, upside down, on his hands, with his body finely arched and the muscles of his back sharply defined, for a period, and then let his feet spill forward as he craned his neck, so his feet hovered just above his head. He was in the "scorpion" posture, a position which he maintained for twenty minutes, after-which he lowered his feet so their soles rested fully on the top of his head. This posture he was quite prepared to maintain for some time, but that he was interrupted by a knock at the door.

"*Avanti*," he said, quickly bouncing back to a normal standing position.

Di Quaglio walked in.

"What seems to be the trouble?" the Pope asked, rubbing his left pectoral.

"*Summus Pontifex*," the small man faltered.

"Yes yes, what is it?"

"Although it pains me—Although I am hesitant to report the matter, seeing that it directly involves your residence, I do not see that I have a choice."

"Go on," the Patriarch of the Western Church said, knocking a cigarette from a pack which sat on the table and proceeding to light it.

"As per your instructions I have been monitoring all telephone calls to and from the Vatican, particularly those connecting to your outer offices. You requested me to inform you of anything out of the ordinary, or of a subversive nature."

"I did."

"There have been such calls."

"That threaten my person?"

"Not through bodily harm, but through proximate taint."

"By whom and to whom?"

"By . . . By the Secretary of State, Cardinal Zuccarelli."

"And to?"

"To a number of different sources."

"Such as?"

"I have prepared a list."

"Let me see it."

"As Your Holiness wishes."

The Pope took the sheet of paper from the other's hand and perused it.

"800-SNM-XXXX," he read.

"I am afraid so, *Summus Pontifex*," Di Quaglio sighed.

"800-FOT-TERE."

"Quite shocking."

"And this other number: 57-555-12. It has been called dozens of times. Is there a reason that it is on the list?"

"Unfortunately, yes. It is—I looked into it personally. It is the number of a kind of escort service."

"Escort service?"

"Yes, Your Holiness. An escort service is a variety of business, most improper, in which a lonely man, or sometimes woman, may, for monetary compensation——"

"Yes yes yes," the Pope said impatiently, with a wave of his hand. "I know what an escort service is. I require details, not definition."

"Certainly, Your Eminence, details: This establishment, run by one Signora Gemma Lombardo, is, from what information I can glean, quite notorious amongst a certain breed of Romans. It specialises in renting out women—Renting out women for a man's most base deeds."

"You are referring to the act of human coitus?"

"I do not dare give it such a tame appellation."

"So?"

"So . . ."

"It is not merely sex?"

"No. Not merely sex, *Summus Pontifex*. Perversions."

"I see. Very troubling."

"It gets worse."

"Do tell."

"These creatures, these slinking harlots from the house of Lombardo;—Oh, but excuse my language!"

"No, please, do not apologise. It adds the necessary colouring to your discourse. Feel free to use what adjectives you will."

"Thank you. As I was saying: These nasty, slinking harlots from the house of Lombardo have been seen entering the Holy residence, in the dark of night, sometimes singularly, but often enough in droves. They gain admittance through the private door near the Sala del Trono."

"Through my private door? In droves? Who has seen them?"

"Both *L'Osservatore Romano* and *Il Giornale* have had anonymous reports sent to them. Each paper was kind enough to refrain from printing them, since their existences largely depend on Your Holiness's will, and simply forwarded the information to me. However, should such reports continue to get abroad, I cannot guarantee that they will be contained. As you know, we have many enemies, and many newspapers would not only be willing to print such information, but would pay for the privilege."

"This is ridiculous!" the Pope cried, crushing the half-smoked cigarette violently in an ashtray. "What are my Swiss Guards there for? Cannot they keep out the whores?"

"As it stands they are under instruction to obey the orders of Zuccarelli, him being the Secretary of State. The Pontifical Swiss Guard, the Guardia d'Onore, the Papal Gendarmes and the Guardia Nobile are all under his jurisdiction. Only with specific orders to the contrary, coming from yourself alone, can they bar that gentleman's guests from entering."

"At least their silence, the silence of the guards who witnessed these harlots can be depended upon?"

"Implicitly, *Summus Pontifex*. Every person of the one hundred Swiss guards has been handpicked from the cream of Swiss Catholic youth and, aside from being nearly physically perfect, come with extraordinary testimonies of character."

The Primate of Italy, after donning his vestments, put a fresh cigarette in his mouth, lit it, and puffed thoughtfully.

"Then who did these anonymous reports come from?" he asked.

"The quartermaster of the guards, who is absolutely devoted to you, told me that, on one occasion, his men saw Cardinal Gonzales parading the zone of the Sala del Trono around the same time that the slinking harlots were admitted."

"Gonzales is not a friend."

"I am afraid not, *Summus Pontifex*."

"He is not loyal. Given the opportunity, he might act in a base fashion."

"I am afraid so, *Summus Pontifex*."

The Pope stood silent, gazing at Michelangelo's fresco of *The Last Judgment*, ranged over his desk; of devils dramatically dragging the souls of the damned down to hell—an infernal and painful hell, where naked men suffered and, together with their partners in sin, burned.

"A most disheartening situation," Di Quaglio ventured.

"Yes; thank you," the Pope said curtly, and began striding around the room. "Worry yourself no more. Mention this to no one. I will take care of the problem."

Di Quaglio, knowing himself to be dismissed, bowed deeply and departed silently.

During the next four hours no one was admitted to see the Pope accept Lucio, who was continually delivering cups of espresso, and the Swiss Guard Betschart, who was instructed to bring in a fresh carton of cigarettes. Clouds of smoke rolled out from the throat of the successor of Saint Peter, curled out from his lips and nose, rising to the frescoed ceiling, and polluting, undermining the work of Ludwig Seitz and all his successors in restoration. It was apparent that the indecorous information the Pope had received troubled him to no small degree.

"This Zuccarelli seems to think we are living in the time of the Borgia," Pope Lando murmured to himself. "He fancies himself to be in the entourage of Alexander VI, and dancing in the Ballet of the Chestnuts, when the city's whores and the personnel of the Vatican competed for orgasms while crawling amongst the candles, effeminate servants crying out their scores to my lecherous predecessor. But in these days of literacy, when newspapers and words are more dangerous than poison or daggers, discretion is the key—A discretion I recommended—A recommendation that has been ignored."

He gazed up at Botticelli's fresco of Sixtus II and took a long drag at his cigarette.

"What a stupid expression the painter gave to this fellow," he said to himself. "Compared to *The Punishment of Korah*, over yonder, this bit of work is really ridiculous. Botticelli obviously did not respect Sixtus II. Yet Zuccarelli respects me infinitely less!"

He turned quickly and strode towards the door. "I will reach my method while walking in the garden," he murmured. "The circulation in this room is not quite what I would wish for."

With an air of incontestable grandeur he walked through the Capella di San Pio V and along the lavishly decorated halls, his legs moving beneath his soutane with their accustomed long, virile strides. He walked along the edge of the Cortile del Belvedere, and stopped briefly to watch a group of Swiss Guards as they played football. The finely built men, thoroughly keen on the game, shouted with joy. The ball was kicked in the vicinity of the Pope. He picked it up and kicked it back, into the centre of the court. The men cheered and threw their fists into the air. Lando smiled benevolently and then departed. Their Swiss-German accents appalled him.

He made his way to his private gardens, the Boscareccio, situated between the zecca and the Viale del Museo, which was the only place in the Vatican he could walk undisturbed. He blinked his eyes as he stepped into the full light of day and breathed in the heavy Roman air. He made his way through the vegetable gardens and grape vines, which were lush and green with summer growth. At the Leonine tower he stopped and, from the terrace, gazed out over the Valle dell' Inferno whose historic brickworks once provided the building material for the whole of Rome. These walks, these places, had been the scenes of a thousand glories and tragedies. The earth of these gardens was fertilised with the blood of ages.

Turning to his left he moved on, to the cool shade of the oak grove, with its marble blocks and pillars, the remains of the bygone empire placed tastefully about. The coloration of the flowers, the purple queen and Chinese foxglove, combined with the ancient spirit of the oaks, soothed him somewhat; but it was with decided aversion that, upon turning a bend, he saw the back of a young man who was seated on a fallen Doric pillar.

"Can I not have any privacy, even in my own garden," he muttered, approaching the figure with every intention of sending him out of his sanctuary.

"Excuse me," he began.

The young man turned. It was Dario, one of Vivan's playmates, his eyes red and his countenance especially pale. He looked distraught and unwell.

"Oh, excuse me," he said, rising in embarrassment. "I was told by the Cardinal—Excuse me, *Beatissimo Padre*—I was told by the Cardinal, Cardinal Vivan, that I might sit in the garden from time to time."

"He told you an untruth," the Pope said.

"I was just leaving, *Beatissimo Padre*—I will leave then." Dario wiped his eyes.

"You have been shedding tears?"

"Yes."

"Sit back down. I grant you leave to remain in my presence."

"Thank you;—it is so peaceful here." Dario regained his seat.

"May I offer you a cigarette?"

The young man bit his lip, and remained silent, simply staring at the ground.

"What troubles you, my son?"

Dario wiped a fresh tear from one eye. "It is Walter—It is Walter, Holy Father."

"Walter?"

"Yes, you remember. The red-headed boy who was dining with us the other day—the one wearing the fur cape?"

"Ah yes, I remember. An especially shy young man. Vivan seemed to have a particular fancy for him."

"Precisely," Dario pouted.

"Are you jealous of Walter? Is that the problem? "

"No, I am not jealous; not in the least," Dario cried. "If Walter were happy and safe, then I myself would be happy. But as it is, I don't know that he *is* happy—or safe. I don't know where he is."

"He has disappeared?"

"Yes."

The Bishop of Rome sat down near the young man and lit a fresh Parisienne. "And why would he not be safe?" he asked with some concern.

Dario looked up with sad, pleading eyes. "Because," he said softly, pushing his black locks away from his eyes. "Because, *Beatissimo Padre*—" He faltered and looked back at the ground.

"Please," the Pope said gravely, "be straight forward with me. I am of the age of understanding and by unburdening your heart you will do more help than harm."

Dario looked up. His eyes flashed. "Because, Your Holiness," he said. And then in one breath: "Terisio, Filippo and Vittorio are dead and I cannot help but think the same has happened to Walter!"

"Please, take a cigarette." The Pope shook a cigarette out of his pack and repeated his offer. "Please, take a cigarette and be calm."

"Thank you, I will."

"Light it from mine."

"You are too kind, Holy Father."

"Not at all. Now tell me about it. Tell me about Terisio, Filippo and Vittorio. If you can trust anyone Dario, it is me."

"I feel this, Your Holiness. I feel this."

"Proceed."

"It is the cardinal; Cardinal Vivan," Dario said, sighing out a plume of smoke which slowly and smoothly drifted off, up into the old oak branches. "We, all of us boys, knew each other before we came here you know. We were the greatest of friends, and usually sympathised with one another. Walter and myself were particularly close."

"I can imagine."

"Yes, well: When the cardinal discovered us;—it was at Club Plastic . . . On a Wednesday night;—Wednesday is their night for—Well, I will skip over the details of our introduction, if you don't mind. They are not really so delicate as I would like them to be."

"Certainly. Speak as you wish. After all, this is not a confession."

"Yes, well: When the cardinal discovered us, we all thought it the greatest stroke of luck. His gifts and attentions flattered us. He gave Terisio a beautiful watch, bought Vittorio a purple Vespa, Walter a two-seater, and fed and clothed us all lavishly. He was certainly the most generous man any of us had ever met, and by no means ugly."

"One would never know him to be forty-two," the Pope grinned.

"Forty-two!" Dario said with some surprise. "Why, I never imagined him to be much over thirty!"

"I believe he dies his hair."

"Most likely," Dario said, putting one leg over the next and taking a drag of his cigarette. "As I was saying though: he is by no means ugly and, with the grandeur of his office and style of living, he fascinated each and every one of us. I am not from a wealthy family," (looking up, speaking apologetically). "Wealth has the power of overwhelming me, making me go against my better judgement."

"But the deaths: Terisio, Filippo and Vittorio. What of their deaths?"

"Yes. Filippo was first. His body was found floating in the Tiber. He was stabbed thirty-six times. I saw him—I saw him afterwards. He used to have a beautiful figure, but now . . . Ravaged . . . Bloated . . ."

"It is certainly a cruel shame. Generally speaking, it is an unpleasant thing to see one's friends ravaged and bloated. But what makes you connect this gruesome incident to Vivan?"

"I would never have suspected him to be sure, if it was not for what followed: Three days after Filippo had been buried (Walter, Terisio, Vittorio and I all helped to carry the coffin)—Three days after Filippo had been laid to rest, I went up to the cardinal's chamber. I was scheduled to meet him for tea. Us being on terms of such, well, familiarity, I did not wait to be asked to come in after knocking. I simply knocked and walked in. I did not see him. I walked to the bedroom, letting my hands run over the cool bronze of Hercules' chest, while passing through the office. There was a peculiar smell in the room. The velvet coverings to the bed were scattered on the floor. I called out. The cardinal came rushing out of the bathroom, wiping his hands. He looked embarrassed. The towel was red with blood. He closed the bathroom door behind him. I asked what had happened and he said he had cut himself shaving; but for the life of me I could see no wound, and the towel was quite drenched. Vittorio's scarf was lying amongst the scattered bed clothes—I know it was his because I gave it to him for his nineteenth birthday, which had just passed."

Dario's cigarette had burnt down to the filter; a long cylinder of ash still clung to it. The young man's gaze was glassy, distant. A breeze licked through the trees and shepherded him out of his reverie.

"That is the story," he said quietly, looking the Pope in the eyes.

"You did not go to the police?"

"No. My family is from the South of Italy. We don't trust the police."

"But you would like revenge?"

"Yes," Dario said, nodding his head, his black curls springing over his forehead.

XVI

VIVAN walked through the large main doors and into the vast hall. The Pope was standing near the window, smoking a cigarette and looking out towards the Vatican hill and over the gardens. He did not immediately turn around and Vivan, thinking his own presence was not known, coughed.

"Ah, there you are," the Pope said, turning and flicking the ashes of his cigarette on the floor. "I was just admiring the view. The sight of boxwood and ilex trees I find particularly conducive to meditation. But come," he said, gesturing towards a grand table set in the centre of the room, "please sit down. Between us, such old friends as we are, there is no need to stand on ceremony."

Vivan was quick to express his admiration for the table arrangements. The English crockery was in excellent taste, adorned with a marigold pattern which was elegant rather than ostentatious and, though thoroughly antique, conformed to the requirements of modern aesthetics. The numerous vases of flowers decorating the table were arranged to the best possible advantage, filling the air with an intricate perfume, the perfume of rare blooms admixed with a particular striking beauty of blossom. There were magnificent fritillaria interspersed with jasmine and willow branches; alstroemerias in dazzling yellow and chaste white, spiked lobelia and mop-headed, pink hydrangea; water lilies floating in Mesopotamic bowls, and Ming dynasty urns stuffed with sheaves of green wheat.

The two men sat across from each other. The Pope lit another cigarette, at the same time expressing his apologies for doing so.

"Please excuse the smoke," he said to his guest. "It makes the wheels of my mind turn so much more smoothly. It is a pleasure I can scarcely do without."

"No need to apologise," Vivan coughed. "I have grown more used to it since coming to Rome. It seems that all the young men I know are great smokers: Walter, Dario, Terisio: I believe none of them can be happy without a cylinder sticking in their mouths."

The Pope smiled tightly.

"Would you like some refreshments?"

"Oh, please."

The successor of Saint Peter rang a small golden bell which sat on the table. Four thin lads, identical in dress and appearance, with round faces and close-cropped black hair, walked silently in. Two carried between them an enormous bread basket, filled with loaves in the shape of sunflowers, pumpkins and sparrows which they set on the table. Another set down a pitcher of water and a bottle of olive oil in the centre of the table, and a small plate of Parmigiano Reggiano near the

173

Pope. The fourth held a large Celtic bronze pitcher in his arms and, approaching the guest first, filled his glass with wine.

"It's delicious," Vivan cried, tasting the beverage while watching the lad saunter around the enormous table in order to serve the Pope.

"I thought you would like it," the Archbishop of the Roman Province said, watching his own glass fill with the aromatic liquid. "It is an old Bordeaux, an 1893 Lafite Rothschild, mixed with pulverised pinecones, as well as small amounts of mastich and pennyroyal."

"I did not realise you were such a decadent!"

"When occasion presents itself, I am many things."

"Such delightful bread; still warm from the oven! And the taste!" Here Vivan could only express himself adequately by use of that typically Italian gesture: pressing the pinched fingers to the lips and kissing them.

"A simple breaking of fast," the Pope said coolly, pouring a little olive oil on his plate and mopping it up with the wheaten head of a sparrow.

"Oh, but I feel quite honoured you know."

"Well, Vivan, you are my right-hand man so to speak, and you deserve to be treated accordingly. I would not lunch you on dried crusts and water."

"Most considerate of you."

"Not at all. I give you only your just deserts."

Just then a serving boy, extremely pale of skin and with hair so blond that it was almost white, stepped in carrying a silver tray laden with baked ostrich heads. Vivan drank the sight in with his eyes, his nostrils opening wide as the youth bent over his plate, depositing a portion of the cuisine thereon.

174

"It smells delicious," he murmured still gazing, not at the food, but the server.

The youth approached the Pope, but the latter waved him away.

"This sort of thing is a bit too rich for me," the Vicar of Christ Upon Earth said, cutting off a piece of Parmesan cheese instead. "I imagine it will suit you, however, as your tastes are more . . . refined."

"Well, I have been told that my tastes are peculiar," Vivan said, watching the boy mince out of the room. "What light skin the little fellow has," he commented, turning and prodding the ostrich head with his fork.

"An albino from Norway. He does not speak a word of Italian. The other four you saw are identical twins from the south, quadruplets, each deaf and dumb. All my servers are alike unusual," (just then a train of fresh boys began to enter, laden with provisions.) "Ah, here is little Leo from Russia, Piasecki from Minsk and Wong from the Szechuan province of China. Behind him is young Pablo from Buenos Aires, who is, unfortunately, blind. Still, look how well he goes about his business!"

Pablo, for all his lack of sight, was indeed dexterous in handling the dish of oyster and crayfish sausages on lily blossoms. With short, solemn steps he made his way to the table, walked along its edge and, when within a foot or two of Vivan, forked a few steaming morsels onto the latter's plate with silent decorum.

"My God!" Vivan shouted in ecstasy. "What I would not give for these boys! They're delicious, delightful . . . I cannot think of adequate words to describe them."

"They are handsome, are they not?" suggested the Pope, smiling slightly to see his guest begin to lose all pretence of indifference toward the young men's charms.

The servers each deposited a portion of the delicacies they carried on Vivan's plate, though not on the Pope's. Leo had with him wild boar with pine nuts, Piasecki's somewhat thin arms were strained under a great platter of camel's heels in vinegar, and Wong stepped easily, bearing a boiled owl with sweet peppers.

Vivan tasted each with ever-increasing glee, washing the food down with mouthfuls of the strong wine. But no sooner had he sampled one dish than a new one was brought forth: the four mute southerners returned bearing trays of poached partridge eggs, scrambled flamingoes' brains, daisy and pellitory salad, and cockscombs on lettuce. The other boys, in fairly rapid succession, brought in great platters piled high with treats: pasta seasoned with peacocks tongues, lobster, goose and figs, parrots heads with saffron, French peaches with fennel and brandy, roast bear with garlic and rosemary and, finally, carried in by four boys at once, a small porpoise resting on a bed of Tunisian dates and blackbirds.

"What an attractive fish," Vivan gurgled ecstatically.

"We seem to be missing something," the Primate of Italy said. He snapped his fingers at Wong and murmured a few words in an unintelligible tongue. The boy ran off bowing and, two minutes later, returned, carrying a bowl which he set before the host.

Vivan, sucking down a mouthful of porpoise, looked over inquiringly.

"Locusts and honey," Pope Lando explained, dripping a spoonful on his own plate. "We cannot do without the food of John the Baptist."

Vivan snickered and began to lap up a peach in brandy.

"You are fond of music, are you not?"

Vivan wiped his lips. "Oh yes. I love all sorts of music: jazz, blues, country and western. I am very fond of Dwight Oakum."

The Primate of Italy dipped a chunk of bread in honey, saying: "I planned an entertainment, but unfortunately Mr. Oakum was unavailable;—I hope a classical quintet will do."

"Classical? Yes, I find the works of Queen positively inspirational!—*Mamma mia—Mamma mia, let me go!*" Vivan shrugged his shoulders burst out in a high-pitched laugh. It was obvious that he was feeling the effects of the wine.

The Primate of Italy looked at his guest with distaste, picked up the bell from the table and rang it. Instantly five serious, black-haired young gentlemen stepped in. They each carried a musical instrument, violins, viola, cello and bass, and were dressed in tuxedo tops and shorts, which showed off their bold, athletic legs. Vivan gave a little squeal as he swallowed a bite of owl. The five sat off to one side and proceeded to play Mozart's "Eine Kleine Nacht Musik."

One of the young waiters approached the Pope with a silver platter on which rested a slip of paper. The latter took up the paper and read it, just as all the bells of all the churches in Rome began to toll three, forcing the quintet to cease playing. The expression on the face of the Primate of Italy was one of concern.

"You must excuse me," he said, rising from his seat. "It seems that a delegation from Zambia has been waiting for me in the Sala degli Arazzi for the past thirty minutes. The appointment completely slipped my mind."

"You have to go? Oh, what a shame—just when we were beginning to enjoy ourselves."

Pope Lando expressed his apologies and exited.

The music resumed, with the minuet, and Vivan continued to eat, dipping his hands into all the delicacies before him, licking sauces from his fingers and time and again putting his greasy lips to the wine glass. After the rondo, the musicians stopped for a short recess. Vivan clapped his hands and asked that each of the five be served "the fruits of the vine," as he expressed it. While this order was being carried out, the large main doors opened and Dario walked in, dressed in a stylish, close-fitting black suit and looking particularly suave.

"Dario? I did not know you had been invited to lunch!"

"Yes," the young man replied seriously. "The Papa told me to attend."

"There are marvellous dishes here; look at the spread."

"Unparalleled, I'm sure."

"Oh, so am I. It is so nice to be pampered."

Dario took a glass of wine, though he seemed to avoid the food, and Vivan chattered away. Presently the entire waiting staff re-entered, burdened under the weight of massive silver trays capped with gorgeous shining lids. They set the trays on the table, removing those dishes which were already ransacked as they did so. The lids were removed, revealing breathtaking piles of moulded food stuffs.

"They look like statues, don't they?" said Vivan, sticking his head forward.

Dario nodded. "Yes. They seem to be busts."

Cardinal-Priest Vivan, sipping his wine, examined one more closely. It was a most curious dish. The black locks, tentacles of squid, curling over a fine forehead, a boyish brow, a head and shoulders made of minced dormice, the whole seasoned with honey and sesame seeds. A truly gourmet model of effeminate male perfection to be sure. The resemblance suddenly struck him. There could be no mistake—the bust, which rested on a bed of crisp arugula, was of the youth Vittorio. Vivan, setting his glass down unsteadily, upset it and the wine spilled over the table, staining the cloth red. His eyes flashed to the second dish, from which arose a strong, relatively sickening aroma. Made of roasted Botswana mopane worms, dripping with melted butter and constructed with nearly the same level of skill that went into Cellini's *Perseus*, the sculpture bore a striking likeness to Terisio. It had a blistery, waxy appearance and, though undoubtedly tasty, inspired Vivan with profound revulsion. The third plate was piled high with Vittorio, constructed entirely of pâté de foie gras. The chef who had erected this masterpiece in goose liver had undoubtedly studied the works of Lysippus and Myron, for it bore true similarities to those artists' works, with the same graceful elasticity and tridemensionalism as the *Apoxyomenos* and *Discobolus*. The fourth torso, in the image of Dario's good friend Walter, was moulded out of a mixture of ricotta cheese, calves' brains and white radish, the hair, being braided corn silk sprayed with the juice of Syrian plums, was a most ghastly red, particularly in contrast to the milk-white face and neck. It was a moody, idealised portrait, not unlike that in red sandstone of King Mentuhotep IV, of the eleventh dynasty, located in the Gregorian Museum.

Vivan gasped. He was mortified. His face took on a sickly, greenish hue.

"What . . . What is the meaning of this?" he stammered.

"Are you no longer hungry?" Dario asked coolly.

There was no reply. Vivan sat, discomposed and staring at the epicurean busts before him.

Dario twisted his lips and then, snapping his fingers at the musicians, asked Vivan: "Well, in that case, shall we dance?"

Johann Strauss Jr.'s "The Blue Danube" struck up. Dario offered Vivan his hand. The latter, somewhat inebriated by wine, alarmed by the grimly decadent dishes before him, took it and rose. His brain was unable to fully grasp the meaning of the affair. Slowly, and with much decorum Dario led him out to the middle of the room. Like an automaton, Vivan followed his lead. The music surrounded them and each note seemed to carry with it a double meaning and dart, float about like soft but deadly insects, now caressing, now stinging the Cardinal-Priest's ears. He felt the young man's icy fingers clasp his own and looked into the other's eyes which were filled with an intensity that he dared not comprehend. He shifted his own gaze away, towards the door, where he spied the train of waiting staff slowly winding in. They carried no foods, no bottles of rare vintage, but each walked solemnly forward, intent and soldierly. The line wound around the dancing couple, formed a surrounding hedge and then stopped, each youth upright with his hands behind his back.

Vivan's feet ceased moving. Dario released his hands and took a step back.

"What is this?" Vivan cried.

The music stopped. Each member of the waiting staff drew forth from his sleeve a blade, four-sided and deadly—a set of fifteenth-century French rondels with raised median ridges, thin, pierced oval guards and pommels.

"Are you all mad? Are you all mad, I say?!?"

There was silence. The young men stepped forward, in unison, the daggers gleaming in their hands.

"What lunacy is this?" Vivan cried in a quivering voice, turning to Dario.

The latter was silent, stern.

"Dario!"

The young man's face was unmoving, pale and almost inhuman. The waiting staff mechanically advanced another step, their eyes without feeling or emotion.

"What are they doing?!? What are you all doing?"

No one said a word. Vivan turned this way and that, but there was no escape. He felt faint. He was surrounded by handsome young men, each endowed with a blade, long, sharp and vengeful. He who had thrilled to butcher the flower of his affections, prick and bash out their lives, sickened in the presence of suitable justice.

"And you, Dario?" Vivan said, trembling.

Dario unbuttoned his jacket and drew from its inside pocket a small magnificent East Indian poniard, the hooked blade flickering, encrusted with diamonds, rubies and emeralds. He pressed his dry white lips together and looked at the Cardinal-Priest coldly.

Vivan threw himself on the floor at Dario's feet. "I know I have a problem!" he cried, partially rising and embracing the young man's knees. "But I love you all so much. I love you, Dario! Can't you see that? Dammit, I love you!"

Dario twitched. Vivan let out a squeal as his throat was cut, blood gushing over his young avenger's fashionable trousers and hands and flecking his white shirt front. Gasping, Dario stepped back. The body fell to the ground, swimming in an ever-widening pool of gore, the wealth of young men piercing, splashing, going about their business like dogs stripping a carcass bare.

"For Filippo, Vittorio and Terisio," Dario whispered. "For you, Walter."

XVII

ST. PETER'S SQUARE was a sea of humans, sweating in the rich afternoon sun. The forepart was cordoned off and chairs were set up therein where the VIP sat—the rich, those who had made particularly generous donations to the Church, politicians and high-level ecclesiastic officials. Before these was set a stage, with a small body of cardinals seated thereon, including Gonzales, O'Malley and Zuccarelli. On the stage was a podium. To the right of the stage sat the Choir of Apostle St. Paul. Carabinieri were stationed around this area, standing with legs apart, looking menacingly self-important. Beyond them was the surge of humanity, made up in a large part by the sick, the cripples, the mad; those who had come with desperate hope—the hope that Christ Jesus would remove their miseries through his miracles, through the hands of his emissary, Pope Lando the Second. Blind men stood, their heads tilted back, mouths agape. Others, cripple of limb, pressed themselves forward, eyes wild with frenzied optimism. Christian youth, from all parts of Europe, waved banners, shouted and sang, happy to mix with the oppressed and the dispossessed before the eyes of God.

As the time approached for the Pope to make his appearance, Di Quaglio grew apprehensive. He had never seen, in his lifetime, such a torrent of people fill St. Peter's Square. He viewed many of them, those who had come with the mad desire to have their ills cured, little better than anarchists, and was extremely worried that they would cause trouble, or that some assassin would infiltrate their ranks, and find an easy target in the Primate of Italy.

"There are a great many sick in the square tonight," Di Quaglio said to the Pope. "I am not sure you should go out. There are far too many. We can make an excuse. We can say that you are indisposed."

"Tell an untruth? For what reason?"

"The situation out front is almost riotous. There are German teenagers chanting your name while a thousand cripples pound the pavement with their crutches."

"All the more reason to make my appearance."

"But many,—many expect things. The sick seem to think you can help them,—heal them."

"And you have no such faith?"

"No man has more faith in you than I, *Summus Pontifex*," Di Quaglio said seriously. "I am just not sure it is the dignified thing to do—to accommodate the riff-raff."

"The riff-raff, as you call them, need to be ministered to as much as any other social group."

"But there are ministers for that, you are the Pope."

184

"Yes, I am the Pope. I am Lando the Second, the first minister on earth, *Servus servorum Dei,* the Servant of the Servants of God."

He strode away. Near the door that led to St. Peter's Square Marco approached him. His features were soft and sad. He looked miserable.

"The task is taken care of?" the Pope asked.

"Yes."

"And you are making further preparations? You have spoken with her?"

"Yes, we have discussed it."

Marco had a pouting, somewhat taciturn air about him. He was obviously upset. The Pope either did not notice or did not choose to notice his cousin's pathetic state.

Instead he simply nodded his head and stepped through the door. Two Swiss Guards, Betschart and Meier, stood frozen and slightly hip-shot on either side, looking like they were snatched from a painting by Giorgione in their rich uniforms. The choir, upon seeing the Pope, rose from their seats and struck up Caelius Sedulius's delightful hymn titled *A sortis ortus cardine,* their voices angelically spilling forth praises to *Iusu natus es de Virgine.*

Pope Lando the Second stalked onto the stage and up to the podium. He stood still for two minutes, with his head bowed, until the choir completed its song. Those up front, who were seated in the cordoned off area, rose and gave a very tame, well-mannered ovation. Behind them, the poor and sick roared like beasts. Men shouted his name vigorously, spraying spittle on those in front of them. Many raised their hands and spread their fingers wide apart, as if they would grab the heavens. Some tried to push their way through. A few clouds sailed before the sun, their shadows gliding over St. Peter's Square.

The Pope spoke and a hush ran through the people. He began with a formal address dealing with general matters in broad terms. Those immediately before him seemed quite satisfied with the nature of the speech. The women and the politicians smiled complacently. The ecclesiastics looked on gravely, deeply absorbed, or at least feigning to be, in every hint of the language.

Those in the rear, the plebeians who made up the vast majority of those present, were, however, not content with these generalities. They began to grow restless, particularly those who had come with specific grievances which they wildly hoped to be resolved. Occasional cries began to emerge from the back and the sea of people began to stir and push forward, like slowly rising waves.

Pope Lando the Second noticed the unrest.

"I see before me battalions of sinners, an army of sufferers," he said addressing the crowd. "Many of you have been excluded from the joys of life;—most of you surely fear the terrors of death. You have come here, a great number of you capering like harlots, not so much to do your souls good, as to find relief from your miseries."

A good number in the front rows cringed at the word harlot, though a few women smiled knowingly to themselves. They did not in the least mind having a young Pope who spoke so forcefully, and found his language to be rather attractive than otherwise.

"I see that, today, we have sick here in great numbers. They have come seeking ministration from my hands, as from the hands of God the Almighty. You want to be touched by the finger of the Lord and absolved from your heinous sins."

The shout of: "Heal me!" could be distinctly heard shoot out from the crowd.

Cripples, the blind, the possessed, the deaf and the dumb, all found their way to the forepart of the crowd, pressing forward in a hideous swollen mass. The carabinieri, fresh ones appearing on the scene as the situation advanced, interlocked arms and held them back. Those in the VIP section were visibly nervous. A number of women were constantly looking over their shoulders and seemed at any moment prepared to stand up and bolt should the dam break and the flood of sick pour through. O'Malley smiled and fingered his rosary. Zuccarelli looked especially pale and grave. The sky darkened and a few of the VIP women were stripped of their hats by a sudden gust of wind.

The Pope spoke: "*Ipso Deo in illis operante*. With insturmentality there is *miraculum*. In the Book of Daniel three children were lifted from the fiery furnace; in Acts, Saint Peter was delivered from his prison. The holy relics, the mantle of Elias, the body of Eliseus, the handkerchiefs of Saint Paul, are miraculous as are the places, the Temple of Jerusalem, the waters of the Jordan, the Pool of Bethsaida."

A woman shouted out from the crowd: "Heal me!— Oh heal me, precious Lando!"

She flailed herself madly forward, with wild, untame eyes, apparently unaware of her surroundings.

"Let her through," the Pope cried.

O'Malley rose from his seat, swept forward, plucked the woman from the crowd and led her to the stage. It now became manifest that she was blind. O'Malley winked at the Pope as he set the woman before him.

"What troubles you, my child?" the Pope asked solemnly.

"I am blind," she sobbed.

"Such is the fate of man, as it is for the mole of the hill."

"Heal me!" she cried frantically. "I have been blind for ten years. I have spent all my money on doctors, but without it doing any good! Please heal me!"

The Pope replied: "If you had given to the poor what you have wasted on physicians, the true physician would have cured you."

"Oh please, Holy Father," she shrieked. "Pity me; pity me! Heal me!"

The crowd joined in. "Heal her! Heal her!" it shouted frenetically.

The Pope raised his hand. The crowd was silent. The sky grumbled.

"I, as the Successor to Saint Peter, have a duty to go into the whole world and preach the truth to all creation. He that believes will be saved; he that does not believe will be condemned."

"I believe in you, Sir,—I believe!"

The Vicar of Christ Upon Earth bent forward and spat into her eyes. She swooned back and was caught in O'Malley's arms. O'Malley chuckled, his thin Irish lips pressed together in a grin. The woman trembled and then, rousing herself, found her feet. She put her hand to her forehead and blinked, rapidly bat her eyelashes.

"I can see! I can see!" she shouted hysterically, flailing her arms in the air. "I can see the light! I can see it clearly now!"

Zuccarelli twisted uncomfortably in his seat. He was suspicious of the proceedings but also touched by the woman's zest. He, however, as a highly suppressed individual, did not care for the public display of emotions. He watched as O'Malley led a young, long-haired man, impaired with crutches, onto the stage. Tears flowed over his cheeks and, in a choked voice with a heavy Sicilian accent, he told of his infirmity and begged the Pope to interfere for him—to speak to the higher powers on his behalf and beg for their kindness.

The Pope turned towards the crowd, raised his hands in the air, and spoke in a commanding voice:

"All holy martyrs, Saint Sylvester, Saint Gregory, Saint Ambrose, Saint Augustine, Saint Jerome, Saint Martin, Saint Nicholas; all holy bishops and confessors; all holy doctors, Saint Anthony, Saint Benedict; all holy priests and levites; all holy monks and hermits, Saint Mary Magdalen, Saint Agatha; all holy virgins and widows; all holy saints of God, intercede for us. Be merciful."

He touched the young man and the latter fell back. The crutches fell away. He rose, brushing his hair from before his eyes, and began to jump up and down, wildly upon the stage like a pathetic, disturbed child.

"I'm free!" he cried, leaping. "I am free of sin!"

Gonzales averted his gaze in disgust. He had seen similar scenes in America and Africa and to him it stunk of fanaticism. Certainly it attracted one desperate portion of the populace, but, in general, it scared the better sort of people away. He pursed his lips together and watched O'Malley snatch another case from the crowd.

This time it was a woman, with a nest of salt and pepper hair done up in a bun on her head, and a young man. The woman prowled up to the stage, dragging the young man behind her. He was a lumbering, oafish sort of fellow, probably around sixteen years old. His body was enormous and his neck as thick as a woman's waist. He stared around him with the wild, dumb eyes of an animal.

"He has the devil in him!" the woman shouted. "My son has the devil in him!"

The boy's hair was in disarray; his mouth dropped open and a thick, swollen tongue lolled out. He looked like a hunted animal: scared and dangerous. The Pope approached, and the boy, wheeling his tongue over his chin, backed off, cowering.

"Careful now," O'Malley warned.

The Pope nodded.

"What is your name?" he asked.

The boy did not answer, but merely wrinkled up his nose.

"Tell me by some sign your name!"

The young man sprang up on tiptoe and craned his thick neck. The veins and tendons protruded, giving it the texture of an oak trunk. His eyes were glaring with madness. "*Baahhh!*" he answered in brutal cry. "*Bahh-Baau! Baau zophesamin anro mainyu!*"

O'Malley stepped up and cautiously hooked a microphone to the boy's shirt.

"*Baau! Baau zophesamin anro mainyu!*" the boy repeated, the perfect Syriac flowing from his lips, without the absence of either sibilant or aspirate.

Whispers ran through the crowd. "He is possessed of the devil," people said to one another. A good many shed tears. Some broke down and fell to their knees in prayer. A few old men, who stood off to one side, chuckled and nudged each other. They considered it a good show, but were pessimists at heart. The woman, the mother with her anguished face and bun of salt and pepper hair, clenched her fists and shook them in the air.

"My son has the devil in him," she shouted. "Free him! Free him from the devil!"

The crowd took the key, especially that overwhelming section of enthusiasts, who valued the outward show of religion far more than silent sanctity. They waved their hands in the air, danced and shouted, repeating the mother's words: "Free him! Free him from the devil!"

The sky was now thoroughly overcast, a rolling mass of black clouds, and though it was only three in the afternoon it felt like early evening. The scene was dramatic. The ocean of people swelled and pitched in the vast St. Peter's Square. The great dome, the dome of St. Peter's Basilica rose up almost fiercely into the conspiring storm.

Di Quaglio hurried up to the Pope and whispered in his ear. "*Summus Pontifex*," he said. "I beg you to consider your position. This is neither the time nor the place to deal with this woman and her depraved son. In all probability they are both mad. You are frightening people!"

The Pope, however, did not heed the sub-prefect's words. Pushing him aside he approached the boy.

Pope Lando the Second, the Vicar of Christ Upon Earth, cried out in a powerful voice: "Almighty Father, who consigned the apostate tyrant, your other son, to the flames of hell; hasten to our call for help and snatch from ruination and from the clutches of the midnight fiend this human being made in your image and likeness. Strike terror, Lord, into the beast now laying waste to your vineyard. Let my mighty hand cast him out of your servant."

People were visibly touched; the air seemed to become suffused with a supernatural perfume; the clouds, which had been gathering overhead, rumbled. One woman, surprisingly enough the wife of the mayor, who sat in the third row, began to whine that she felt the Holy Ghost inside herself.

Pope Lando the Second, the Successor of Saint Peter, made the sign of the cross on the brow, lips and breast of the boy.

"We cast you out, you onslaught of the infernal adversary!" he said in a voice quivering with grave authority. "We command you, begone and fly far from the precious blood of the Divine Lamb. The bones of the martyrs command you. Give way to the holy apostolic Church!"

He pressed his fingers rather violently to the boy's forehead and the boy began to shake as if he were working a jack-hammer. He flailed his arms and neighed. Di Quaglio, fearing he might attack the Pope, summoned Betschart and Meier, the two Swiss Guards, who ran onto the stage, quaintly ridiculous in their sixteenth century style outfits of black, red and yellow. The three men together, with the utmost difficulty, restrained the young man.

The Pope continued:

"May the trembling that afflicts this human frame, the fear that afflicts this image of God, descend on you. Make no resistance nor delay in departing from this young man. Use him no longer as your vessel. Do not think of despising my command because you know me to be a great sinner. It is God Himself who commands you. God the Father commands you; God the Holy Spirit commands you. The blood of the martyrs commands you. The continence of the confessors command you. Depart, then, transgressor. Depart seducer, full of lies and cunning, foe of virtue, persecutor of the innocent. I now and this moment adjure you, profligate dragon, in the name of the spotless Lamb, who has trodden down the asp and the basilisk, and overcome the lion and the dragon, to depart from this boy. Depart from the Church of God!" He made a sign to the crowd. "Tremble and flee, as we call on the name of the Lord, before whom the denizens of hell cower, to whom the heavenly Virtues, Powers and Dominations are subject, whom the Cherubim and Seraphim praise with unending cries as they sing: Holy, holy, holy, Lord God of Sabaoth!"

The boy lapped frantically at the air. His eyes were bloodshot. The mother, several strands of her salt and pepper hair now disengaged from the bun, clenched her fists before her eyes and moaned with savage emotion.

The Pope's voice trembled with an oratorical flourish, "It is hard for you to kick against the goad. The longer you delay, the heavier your punishment shall be; for it is not men you are condemning, but rather Him who rules the living and the dead, who is coming to judge both the living and the dead and the world by fire. Give place to the Holy Spirit, who by His blessed apostle Peter openly struck you down in the person of Simon Magus; who cursed your lies in Annas and Saphira; who smote you in King Herod because he had not given honour to God; who by his apostle Paul afflicted you with the night of blindness in the magician Elyma, and by the mouth of the same apostle bade you to go out of Pythonissa, the soothsayer."

The boy, still shaking violently, fell to the ground where he writhed for a few moments and then threw up a sticky, brightly hued and unpleasant substance, his face pale and eyes blazing.

"Mamma," he said, tears flowing from his eyes. "Mamma!"

"It's gone, it's gone!" the woman shouted in a frenzy. "The devil is gone from my boy!"

She grasped the arm of the massive, ape-like child and helped him up. His face was white, but he smiled. He scratched himself and waved to the audience. A thrill ran through them.

The entire crowd was ecstatic, those in the VIP section certainly no less so than the others. Women, well positioned in society, rose from their chairs and shouted praises to God, Lando the Second and the Church, though in varying order. They cared not if they compromised themselves by their unseemly behaviour: the Spirit was in them and they could not help but let it manifest in gyrations of their hips and untame, hyena-like cries.

The Pope, the Vicar of Christ Upon Earth, gazed gravely over his flock. He stepped forward, his finely wrought features distinct, even from a distance. A rumbling came from the darkened sky and wind swept through St. Peter's Square.

He spoke:

"You wanted divine mysteries, now smell their incense; you want divine union: have it!—Hear my Bull and be baptised in its blood!—Feel the Holy Ghost!"

He flashed his hands forward, rapidly opening the fingers as if flecking the audience with water. They surged back, as if struck by a powerful wave. The first three or four rows of people fell to the ground, in a simultaneous swoon, where they quivered and shook with spasms.

"The Holy Ghost has me! The Holy Ghost has me!" one man shouted at the top of his voice. A woman writhed wildly on the ground like a severed worm.

"I feel His Love!" she shrieked. "He is giving me His Love!"

At this point it began to rain; first just a few drops came down, large and scattered. People raised their hands up towards the heavens as if they were receiving a blessing. The fanatical youth turned back their heads and stretched forth their tongues, as if for the sacrament. The drops fell more briskly. The old men ran for shelter. The rain thickened, grew to a torrent and began to soak and partially disperse the crowd.

"It is a baptism," some said in reverent voices. "It is a Holy Baptism!"

Gonzales stalked away to his chambers, thoroughly sickened by this ostentatious display of religion. If ever there was a false prophet, he told himself, Lando the Second was it.

"The man seems to be a specialist at mass hypnotism," the old cardinal hissed between his teeth.

There was no question in his mind that the face of the Church was changing, changing rapidly and for the worse.

The next day, the majority of news services exaggerated rather than reported the events. One Catholic paper said that, previous to the storm, the sun had appeared to be suffused with blood, and many stars were visible in the daylight. Another boldly asserted that orange-flavoured rain had fallen from the sky, while a third spoke of "a shower of pearly golden corpuscles." In general, the consensus was that there had been an unexplainable atmospheric phenomenon.

XVIII

"NO, I have not seen him. Did you check the Sala degli Arazzi?"

"I have checked everywhere. The Pope is now utilising Di Quaglio as his secretary, but I cannot get any information from the latter as to how he arrived at the situation, whether it is permanent or merely temporary. No one has seen or heard of Vivan for the past week. He has simply disappeared. It is as if someone had kidnapped or done away with him."

"Yes, I can understand how you might think it a bit queer," O'Malley said with a somewhat forced smile. "But things have changed since Alexander VI's time. We don't go in for heavy intrigues these days."

"But the last he was heard of was when he was lunching with the Pope," Zuccarelli pointed out.

"Oh, come now Cardinal," O'Malley laughed, putting his hand on the other's elbow. "The lad is probably simply visiting his mother and doesn't want to be bothered. He was always one for his mother and, if I were a betting man, that's where my money would lie,—on him sitting around at his mother's place for a spell and fattening up on her fine cooking."

Half satisfied with this explanation, Zuccarelli nodded his head, expressing his hopes that the case were thus as well as his intention to investigate and determine if it were so.

"Well, give the lad my regards when you see him," O'Malley said. "Tell him he's missed at Vatican City."

Zuccarelli, in an extremely pensive state of mind, made his way back to his own chambers, through the Portone di Bronzo and along the Scala Pia. He took a key from his pocket, opened the large oak door to his sanctuary, and stepped in. The first room was an outer office. He sat down at his desk and called the telephone information operator in Padua.

"I want the number for a Signora Vivan, in Padua—Yes, as it is the only one listed it is bound to be right. Thank you."

He called the number and asked the old woman if her son was at home.

"At home, here?" she cried. "I have not heard from him for nine days! And he usually calls me every Friday, Sunday and Wednesday! He is such a good boy; he simply cannot have forgotten me."

She then went on to explain that she herself had been to the police, but they swore they could do nothing unless he had been missing for a longer period of time. She had called the Vatican and numerous officials, but always with unsatisfactory results. She had even tried to contact the Pope, but without luck.

"Please, see if you can find him," she begged. "The sheer worry is breaking my heart!"

"Yes, certainly," Zuccarelli replied, in agitation. "I will do everything I can to locate him."

He lay down the receiver.

"*Fava della Madonna!*" he murmured. "This is no good!"

That his destiny was somehow linked with Vivan's was a fact he readily acknowledged. As dominant ecclesiastics they had lived in Padua, often strolling and dining together; mutually targeted by Torturo, they had risen in unison. Torturo, as Pope Lando the Second, was capable of anything—Zuccarelli was sure on that score. If Vivan was damned would he, Zuccarelli, be?

He thought not.

"I believe it is time to put a little distance between myself and Rome," he said to himself. "There is no reason why necessity cannot impel me to make a sudden trip to Austria—or Sweden, let's say . . . I will pack my bags and be off. If Vivan turns up and the whole thing is a false alarm, then I can always return;—But if not, if my suspicions are correct . . ."

Without giving himself time to finish the thought, he swept into his bed chamber.—In half an hour he could have his bags packed and be on his way to the train station.—He stepped to the maple dresser, opened it and removed his white linen suit, deciding it would be best to travel incognito. He sat down on the antique, four-poster bed which was placed square in the centre of the room, the walls of which were frescoed entirely red, with black trees upon which hung numerous fruits in the shape of naked men and women, twisted in immodest postures. He bent down and began to unlace his shoes.

"Do you have a rendezvous somewhere?"

The cardinal looked up. Clara was standing at the sitting room entrance. She was dressed in a tuxedo top, black shorts and black fishnet stockings, her feet sheathed in black, high-heeled leather boots. A large snakeskin purse hung from her shoulder.

"Yes. I was getting ready to go out.—How did you get here?"

"I just put one hoof in front of the other."

"I mean into my rooms."

"Why? Aren't you glad to see me?"

"I have an appointment in Munich; I don't have time for . . ."

"You don't have time to be naughty?"

"Un—unfortunately not—I would love to, but unfortunately not."

She stepped up to him, her cellulose thighs bulging monstrously and stretching the shorts taut.

"Don't you want to suffer?" she asked, pinching his chin. "Are you angry with me?"

"No, I am not angry—but I don't have time."

Clara slapped him briskly on the cheek.

"Don't you want to suffer!" she screamed.

"Yes—please, hurt me!" he burst out, throwing his arms around her waist and burying his face in her bosom. It was too difficult to resist the heat of her person, those fatty thighs sheathed in black fishnet.

"You old pervert," she laughed, kneeing him away. "Here, put this on," she said, reaching into her purse and pulling out a garment—a dress, like those worn by German housewives, of a sickly, greenish hue.

The cardinal deftly slipped out of his cassock and into the dress.

"You look charming."

"Oh, Clara," he said, falling to his knees.

"Call me Sir."

"Yes, Sir."

She kicked him.

"Will you be good?"

"Yes;—Yes, Sir."

Clara took a blindfold and coil of rope from her bag.

"Get up," she said.

The cardinal rose to his feet and stood, tall and thin, his pale, hairy legs sticking awkwardly out of the frock. His face, with its hawk's nose and penetrating eyes, looked rather serious, despite the ridiculous costume he had been made to wear.

Clara smiled wickedly at him. She tied the blindfold over his eyes.

"Can you see?" she asked.

"No. Not at all. Nearly not at all."

"Good."

Gently humming a romantic air, she began to tie his wrists together behind his back, with all the adept skill of a sailor. As he felt the sturdy ropes wind around his wrists, bind him, and smelled her perfume, Musk Koublai Khan, that never failed to thrill, all thoughts of worry truly slipped from his mind. His delectation provoked, he could only, like an animal, experience the present moment.

"That feels wonderful," he murmured when the ropes were fixed.

201

"Do you like it?"

"Very much."

"Good. Now bend over."

He did as he was told.

"Good girl."

"Am I?" he asked.

"Yes. You are being a very good girl."

He lay one cheek on the floor, proned his rump in the air and attempted to peer through the edge of his blindfold. He could see nothing, but could hear movement.

"I can see your fanny," she said

He laughed.

"Ready?"

"Yes," he replied in an unsteady voice.

A jolting pain hurdled through him, from the back forward. He screamed. The pain came again, with re-doubled force, surging from his buttocks and through his spine like a galvanic shock.

"My God, you are rough today!" he cried.

"Don't you like it rough?"

"Yes, but——"

"Don't you like it rough?"

"Yes, I do."

"Yes, what?"

(He felt a boot press against his spine.)

"Yes, Sir. I like it rough, Sir."

There was a cough.

"Who is that?"

"Oh, it's just me."

"And that smell? Are you smoking?"

"Yes."

"Then——"

Zuccarelli was about to make further comment, but, before he could, a brisk and incredibly powerful blow was delivered to his rear end, which sent him sprawling forth on the floor howling. Several more came, in rapid succession; potent, painful, sadistic. The dress was ripped from his shoulders and he felt a blow across his naked back. He clawed his way forward, like a hunted animal, until he reached the wall. Raising a shivering hand to his face, he partially tore away the blindfold. Through the corner of an eye he thought he discerned a strip of white retreating through the door.

"Who was that?" he mumbled.

"A surprise, you naughty boy."

Clara kneeled down next to him, petting his head and kissing his eyes and neck.

"Don't you like surprises?" she teased.

"I must say, I am surprised at your strength. My nether region aches atrociously. Have you been going to the gymnasium?"

"Do you want your surprise, mousy?" she asked, ignoring his question and petting him amorously. "You want to *feel lovely*? Do you want your surprise, mousy?"

"I suppose so," he replied, the soft dominance of her hand thrilling him. "Yes; I suppose I do."

"Girls," she said, rising and turning around. "Girls!" she called, clapping her hands.

The door to the sitting room opened. Three women walked in. One, slim, blonde, apparently in her early

twenties was dressed in a pink leather policeman's out-
fit, the only difference being that the legs, encased in
white net hose, were exposed. She carried a blue leather
whip with a beaded handle which she cracked in the
air. Her lips were cruel and of an extreme, artificial red,
which glistened like a bloody wound on her face.

The second was about forty years of age and quite
heavy, with flaming, curly red hair which reached down
to her derrière. Her clothing was of tight black silk
with black, leather strips bound impromptu around
her arms and thighs, her pale, white flesh curling up
around them. Her tool was a riding crop which she
wielded, swatting her palm meaningfully. Her breasts,
which oozed out of her clothing, were over-ripe and
her swollen lips appeared veterans of unnatural vice.

The third woman, scarcely twenty years of age, had
straight black hair cut short and a pleasing, calm face
which was made somewhat extraordinary by a set of
sky-blue eyes which stared vacantly before her. Her
skin was as white as paper, aside from a small patch on
her neck which was raw and pink. Dressed simply, in
tight black trousers and a red T-shirt, she carried two
burning tapers, one in each hand.

"Let me introduce you," Clara said with a smile.
"Gina, Gabriella and Temple."

"Very nice," he said, shifting on his knees.

Gina gave a contemptuous sneer at the elderly
man, his chest rife with grey hair and the nostrils of
his noble, aquiline nose flaring with obvious desire.
Gabriella laughed, her hefty bosom jiggling. Temple
stared blankly at him, as if he were no more than a piece
of furniture, rather than a naked, lust-filled cardinal.

Zuccarelli gave Gabriella a pleading look. She smiled at him, showing a set of glistening white teeth, slightly smeared with lipstick.

"I see you like Mistress Gabriella?" Clara laughed.

"Yes."

"What is it you like about her?"

"Yes, what is it you like about me?" Gabriella lisped in Venetian dialect.

"I like your hair, Gab—Mistress Gabriella."

"You like sluts?" she lisped. "Do you like fat girls?"

"Yes. I like fat girls." His chin trembled.

"Are you a *stallone*?" she asked, approaching him. "Are you a stallion?"

"I will be . . . If you want me to, I will be." He chewed at his bottom lip.

She straddled his back and struck him in the side with the crop. He laughed weakly. He felt her full flesh, her weight intense, as if it were about to break his spine in two. He groaned with obvious satisfaction. She laughed wildly.

Gina shrugged her shoulders impatiently. She sneered with undisguised contempt at the spectacle.

"Gina," Clara said. "Go ahead, Gina."

"As you want."

The young woman, standing hip-shot, cracked her whip, the tip of it just nipping Zuccarelli's ear. A single drop of blood fell to the ground. He gave a little scream of mingled excitement and pleasure. Gina's face was stolid. She raised her eyebrows slightly.

Gabriella struck him on the neck with the riding crop, accompanying the gesture with a violent, predatory cry. Zuccarelli screamed and bucked in consternation.

"Do you like that?" Gabriella asked mildly.

"My God," he replied. "It's too rough!"

Clara laughed. "Get off him, Gaby," she said. "He's a string bean. You're too heavy for him."

Chuckling and smacking her hungry lips Gabriella dismounted. Gina, still standing with complete composure, flicked the whip, again nicking his ear.

"Too rough!" he cried in a somewhat demanding voice.

"See, he's a man," Clara laughed.

"So he is," Gabriella said and pinched his cheek.

He smiled and looked up at Temple. He wondered when she would join the game. She batted her eyelids and opened her mouth slightly, but otherwise showed no awareness of her surroundings. He suddenly found her immensely attractive. Her abnormally white skin, the stupid vacancy of her face and the coolness with which she viewed the cardinal's degraded position was more than enough to inflame his desire.

Gabriella was the most active. She would not leave the cardinal alone. She smacked him, pinched him and was constantly circling him, pressing her heaving flesh up against his gaunt, kneeling figure.

"You like this?" (Hitting him on the backside with her riding crop.)

He squealed with delight. "Oh, yes!"

She struck him on the shoulder and he cried out in pain. She struck him again, this time much harder and put her boot against his chin. Pushing his head back with her heel, she struck him savagely on the throat.

206

"Stop!" he cried, gasping for air. He did not mind the humiliation, but felt that the pain was getting to be a bit too extreme. He rubbed his neck while Gabriella loomed over him, caressing the handle of her riding crop.

"Is she rough *schiavo*?" Clara smiled. "Is she too rough, slave?"

"Yes. Please. Tell her to stop."

"Would you like Temple to help you?"

"Yes. Please." (Looking up at the young, pleasant-faced woman with pleading eyes.)

"Temple," Clara said. "Go ahead, Temple."

Temple did not reply. She minced forward, the tapers waving in her hands, kneeled down near the cardinal and kissed him on the cheek. His mouth became moist with delight and he murmured a few words of pleasure. After the rough strokes of Gabriella he found the feathery touch of Temple extraordinarily agreeable. She bat her eyelids vacantly and then, raising the tapers above the cardinal, began to slowly drip wax on his naked back, letting it build until a few drops slid down his side.

"That feels superb," he murmured.

She said nothing. In the puddle of soft, hot wax that had formed on his back she placed one candle. Meanwhile Gina strutted before him, occasionally adjusting her blonde hair, fingering her whip, the pink leather of her costume tight about her and glistening as if wet. Temple kissed his neck. Gina, obviously eager to make him suffer, cracked her whip quite near his face.

"Keep her away," he said. "Keep Mistress Gina away."

"You like Temple more?" Gabriella asked.

He did not answer.

"You like Temple more?" Clara asked, her words hard.

"Yes, she is more gentle," Zuccarelli said, delighted with the role he was playing. Nothing pleased him more than to be like a submissive dog before these dominant women.

"Temple," Gabriella said, handing her a jar.

Temple, placed her second taper between her pressed together thighs, and, taking the jar, emptied a portion in the palm of one hand. She began to rub the jelly on the cardinal's shoulders, down to the middle of his back, where the candle burned upright.

"Very nice," he murmured. "This ointment is very nice."

Gabriella winked at Clara. Gina strutted about impatiently, with a saucy, contemptuous look on her beautiful face.

"What a wonderful evening," Zuccarelli purred; and then, looking up at Temple: "Rub my body, ma'am."

The young woman gazed at him with her limpid blue eyes, blinked and dispensed more of the jelly onto her palms; she proceeded to rub his neck and head and saturated his close-cropped hair.

"Very nice indeed," he murmured. "What is it?"

"Temple!" both Clara and Gabriella said simultaneously.

The young woman took the taper from between her thighs and, calmly, looked at Zuccarelli, her extraordinary sky blue eyes without emotion.

"It has a familiar odour, like——"

Gina gave a frigid little laugh.

"Temple!" Clara shouted.

"Fuel," the cardinal said, raising himself on his elbows. "It smells like some kind of gas."

"Temple!"

With just the flicker of a smile, the young black-haired woman set the flame of the candle to his hair, lighting it, turning it into a blazing crown that quickly flashed down his neck and back as he leapt to his feet. He arched his spine, letting out a horrendous, pain-laden scream. For a moment, a brief instant, he caught sight of himself in the mirror opposite, his eyes rolling red balls, his lips pulled back to the roots of his gums and a shivering tongue stretching forth.

While Temple herself was silent, as she had been since her entrance, the other three women were fully indulging in laughter, both Clara and Gabriella, uncontrolled, uproarious; Gina with a sinister giggle, her top teeth showing like pearls over the vermilion of her bottom lip, which she bit. He was suffering terribly, this lecherous old cardinal, and finally she showed signs of satisfaction.

"Quick!" Clara cried, pointing towards the restroom door. "Into the bath. It is the only way to cool off!"

Zuccarelli leapt rather than ran through the door, his head and back still ablaze, crackling somewhat and sending up a good deal of black smoke. The fleeing soles of his feet disappeared through the entrance to the bathroom. There was the sound of a splash, of a whole body hurling itself into liquid, which was instantly followed by a cry so horrendous, so deafening, that the

women were forced to put their hands over their ears—
and even then they could not make themselves deaf to
the nauseating exhalations of pain. . . . Upon removing
them, those paws adept at vice, the women only heard
a steady sizzling, like garlic sautéing in a pan. An odour,
sulphurous, unpleasant, reached their noses.

"Ooh!" Temple said, moving out of the room. "The
stink is terrible."

XIX

"YOU don't need to worry," he said slowly. "If there is one thing I know it is how—how to do a clean job."

"Believe me, I trust you fully," the Successor of Saint Peter said with a nonchalant gesture of his hand.

There was a minute's silence. The Pope still paced thoughtfully about the room. Marco stood, almost motionless in the same place.

"Please, sit down," the Pope finally said, seeming to just notice that the other was still standing.

"Do you think it was necessary?" Marco asked, remaining upright, but lowering his head.

"Vivan and Zuccarelli?"

"Yes. Do you think it was just?"

The Pope smiled:

"Oh, I think I did them full justice. Really, they got more than they deserved. Instead of being crudely executed, they were done away with in a manner that suited to each his own particular predilection. Mighty generous punishment if you ask me. They indulged in luxury, they forgot God, and were tortured in like manner."

"Yes, but the punishments were far worse than the crimes!"

"Certainly. If the quantity of luxury and deceit fill but a thimble, let the torment fill a barrel. If a man indulge in luxury for one day, his torture should be equal to a whole year. Therefore, for all the crude luxury people indulge in, there is a great deal of torture to be undergone;—if not here, then in the hereafter. If we had left the task undone and not applied the appropriate remedies to these wounds of the Church, then God Himself would certainly have severed the rotten limbs and, as sure as the sun does shine, annihilated them with fire and sword."

"But, don't you consider this work, this theft of human life to be evil?"

Torturo looked steadily at his cousin. "Sometimes God uses evil, or what men call evil, to help along His own wise and mysterious purposes. And, in our case, it is not theft. Their lives were not their own to play folly with."

"But . . . who will be next?" Marco asked with a pained expression. "If you only knew how I felt about the whole thing. I am so sick of dragging corpses around."

"I know you do not like it, cousin."

"When you invited me here, and had me invested—I thought it was for other purposes—I thought that finally my life was to take a more spiritual turn."

"It will, Marco."

"Truly?"

"Yes."

"No more . . . liquidations?"

"No. None;—none that I will have you involved in. You disposed of Dr. Štrekel for me and for that I am perpetually grateful. You have helped greatly with the arrangements for Zuccarelli and Vivan, and carted off their bodies without previous complaint. You are my cousin, but that does not matter, because I refuse to commit nepotism.—What does matter is that you are loyal—You are loyal and as good as gold . . . You have been a priest for six months. You are over the age of thirty, born in lawful wedlock, you have no defects of the mind and, as far as I am concerned, are free from censure. The seat at Padua is open. I will make you a bishop and install you therein. Your only duties will be religious. You are the new Bishop of Padua."

Marco was visibly overcome. "But . . . But don't I need some kind of theological degree?" he murmured.

"It is true that you should be licensed in canon law or theology or, preferably, have the degree of Doctor. But the most important thing is that you are seen fit to teach others and I, the most high authority of your order, declare that you are so fit."

Marco threw his arms around the Pope in joy. "I always told mother she was wrong about you when she said you were wicked," he said, wiping tears from his eyes. "This news will please her tremendously."

"My aim is always to please," Pope Lando said seriously.

Several weeks after this conversation occurred, the Pope paced the length of the Sistine Chapel in restless agitation, his heels ringing against the *opus alexandri-*

num floor. He had a thousand problems to solve, those which were simultaneously the burden and thrill of his office, and his mind never worked at its optimum level in an enclosed space, no matter how grand it might be. That he needed to give free rein to his limbs, let them operate in open, unconfined spaces, was obvious.

He retired to his dressing chamber, poured himself a glass of Chianti and drank it off at a swallow. Casting aside his skull cap, and divesting himself of the white soutane, he dressed in a slightly shabby wool suit, not at all in the latest fashion. He placed the wig upon his head, an unnatural red, slightly curly, covering the entire nape of his neck. He pressed his hand against one of the intricately decorated panels which covered the walls and a small door, dating from the time of Pius IV, opened near the dresser. He walked along the narrow passageway, which, designed by Pirro Ligorio, was meant to be an emergency escape route in times of danger, and wound his way beneath the Sala dei Ministri and the Cortile di San Damaso.

Coming out in the rocks of the Fontana dell'Aquilone, he snuck through the gardens, past the Pontifical Academy of Sciences and around the Leonine Tower. He moved on, through the oaks, past the marble blocks and pillars, and to the great wall which surrounded the Vatican and its precincts. Removing an elaborate gold key from his pocket, he approached a small door, barely noticeable due to the shrubbery which surrounded its vicinity and, after applying the key, opened it, stepped through and breathed in the air of the outside world. He was on the Viale Vaticano. There were a few pedestrians and many cars and scooters. He closed the door behind him, turned to the right and, with ample space to give his long, virile strides the freedom of motion they required, proceeded along the street, unmolested and apparently unnoticed.

It was a beautiful fall day. It was hot. Clouds floated calmly through the blue sky. Tourists manipulated their magnificent, overfed torsos through the streets of the greatest city on earth, balancing precariously on pale, unexercised legs. They wiped the sweat from their foreheads and peered through camera lenses. The Roman shopkeepers stood by, unperturbed in the shade, devoting the minimum amount of effort necessary to life.

The Primate of Italy, in his costume looking more like pimp than Pope, strode along in sanguine spirits. There was little he enjoyed more than walking in the open, without the frenzy of the Vatican around him. The gears of his mind were grinding away, forming and refining plans, vast campaigns: There were a number of people to excommunicate, certain powerful men who threatened his position. The canonico-legal traditions that, in the twenty-first century, made the Church appear almost ridiculous in the eyes of any well-educated person, required drastic reform. The famine-stricken millions in Africa should be tended to. It was time to carve away a bit of the fat from Europe and America and distribute it to the awaiting jaws of the underprivileged. The Bull "Benedictus Deus" which Benedict XII had issued due to John XXII's wishy-washy behaviour needed to be revoked. Both men's notion of the Beatific Vision were absurd in the extreme. The ecclesiastico-

215

political theorists who threatened Europe with their doctrines of separatism and were stoking the fires of non-tolerance and hatred needed to be put in their places. Young, vigorous blood needed to be pumped into the Church and the spoiled, dull old fellows tossed away, composted like used coffee grounds.

"Yes," Torturo thought, sticking his last cigarette in his mouth and lighting it, "there is much work to be done in order to reform this Catholic religion, to return it to its rightful state and make it more than a mere plastic mask."

He walked along the via le Bastione de Michelangelo and, at the Piazza del Risorgimento, turned left, making his way through the small streets that lie between the via Cola di Rienzo and the viale Giulio Cesare. At a newsstand he stopped to buy a fresh pack of Parisiennes. He noticed a familiar looking man buying plums at a fruit seller's just a half a block away. The man was dressed in blue sweatpants, a green shirt, a fishing cap and sunglasses.

"That fellow was walking behind me at Bastione," Pope Lando thought.

Yes, he was being followed, that was obvious.

"Undoubtedly some trick of Gonzales's," he murmured. "He is more clever than I thought."

He walked along the via Caio Mario, turned the corner at the via degli Scipione, advanced a few paces and then stopped.

"We will see what this man wants," he said, grinding his fist into the palm of his hand and smiling.

216

Several seconds passed, but no one turned the corner. Just as he was about to step forward and peer around the edge of the building, the disguised Pope heard a sound behind him. He pivoted. From the alley to his left, an apparent passage to the via Caio Mario, a dark, hulking shape lunged rapidly forth and struck out. The Pope fell, reeling, blinded by a burst of swimming red light. He could feel his fingernails scrape on the brick pavement. He lifted his head. Another flash of pain; his face covered, burning suffocation; and then blackness.

*

"How do you feel?"

He only knew everything was dark and all was throbbing misery.

"How do you feel?"

"Wonderful." The membranes of his nostrils were on fire.

There was silence. Torturo tried to move. He could not. He strained his hands without success. They were apparently tied together, as were his legs.

"You are tied."

"It seems so," he murmured.

"Does your head hurt?"

"Somewhat."

"Good."

He heard a chair move, a door open and close, and then the hollow sound of footsteps receding down a passage. He tried again to move his limbs, but they were secured fast. He could feel that his trousers were wet. He had obviously been left to wallow in his own filth. His head throbbed with pain.

"I have been kidnapped," he murmured. He tried to evaluate the situation, to put together a rapid plan for escape, but his mind was foggy. His thoughts, like untranslatable hieroglyphics, strange logographs, danced before him, refusing to fall into any kind of comprehensive order. Squirming like some underwater creature, a squid or wounded manta, his understanding sank in churning blackness, and receded back into the tunnel of unconsciousness.

When he came to again, water was being poured down his throat, but he was still blindfolded.

"How you feel?"

"Fine."

"How you feel, Patriarch of the Western Church?" (With distinct sarcasm.)

"Fine."

"Do you recognise my voice?"

"I do."

"You do?"

"At first I did not, but now I do."

"You like it?"

"Yes, Doctor. I find your slightly incorrect Italian positively charming."

"I am living."

"That is a comfort."

The blindfold was removed. Torturo blinked and looked around. He was in a moist, windowless room, which was most likely the basement of an old house.

The walls were of unfixed stone, the floor of dirt. The only light came from a tiny bulb over the door. The only piece of furniture in the room was a chair, on which sat the doctor, twisting a strip of cloth, the blindfold, in his hands. He looked the same, except that his huge moustache was now salted with white and his hair, which had been cropped short, was now long and hung down to his shoulders. It too, with a few gray streaks, showed signs of recent stress.

"Good afternoon," he grinned.

Torturo was silent. He tried to manipulate his hands free.

"I am alive," the doctor continued, giving his prisoner a truly evil look. "Your friend: He shot me but did not kill me. He shot my wife and killed her—He killed Žnidaršič . . . But me—the bullet went in my neck and out the side, not even touching the mandible, not touching the carotid. You see," he said, pointing to a scar below his right ear. "You see, it did not kill me!"

The doctor got up, stuffed the blindfold in his pocket and cracked his knuckles.

"What you think?"

"I think that I could endure listening to you much better if I had a cigarette and my hands were free." He knew that, were his hands free, he would have little trouble freeing his body. He was strong and his hands, like Jacob's, were the conduit of his powers.

The doctor wheeled around and, though he was about to kick him in the side, refrained.

"You will listen," he murmured, and resumed his seat. "Your friend, he shot up my family. Deep into the dry well he threw us all. I woke in the rain and felt the breast of my dead wife. My neck was stiff and I felt much pain. Žnidaršič's bloody tongue slept on my cheek. It was night. I called out many times. My voice echoed in the well. No one came. I have no power and go to sleep. Then it was light again. I saw the blue overhead. I called. No one came. I struggled, but fell back. I was hungry and again lost consciousness . . . Then it was once more dark, but I was not dead. I was so hungry. I chewed at Žnidaršič's tongue. It was good, wholesome meat. I eat and sleep. Then it is day again and I spent the time looking at the blue Slovenian sky. I was many days in the hole. I was not ready to depart this life. So I push the dead ones away. I braced my back against one side of the well. I braced my feet against the other. Slowly, I worked my way out;—I am not a stupid incapable man, eh? I have power?"

"Yes, you are a clever fellow."

The doctor gave a short laugh and continued: "I got up to the edge of my well, and climbed out. I staggered to the house. Inside I took notice of my wound. It was a small amount infected. I spilled Russian vodka on it and then drank three glasses of the *teran*. It revived me, restored my vital powers. Out the window I saw the sun coming up;—I was amazed how the time had gone and slipped away! I walked outside, into the courtyard. I looked over and saw movement—When I step nearer I see all my nice pork, moving with white worms. They eat up all my nice pork;—wholesome, Slovenian meat . . . I got Nassa, my wife, out of the well and the dog Žnidaršič. They looked not good—They smell awful—I took them to the field and buried them, deep in the dirt near the vineyard; near the vineyard where I grow my *teran*, the grapes for my black wine. I cried many tears and ripped much hair from my head. I buried them and swore I will make the priest suffer. I will make the priest Torturo suffer and then get his friend, and kill him dead."

Both men were silent. Torturo looked thoughtful, dim.

"What you think?" the doctor asked.

"That you were surely not pleased to see me, the priest, elevated to the highest position."

"Pleased? Oh, it made things more clear. I saw it would make you harder to get at; but the revenge more sugary."

"But, you did manage to get at me."

"Yes. I came. I watched. You like to walk. You told me you did. You are a fit man, and I guessed you would be walking from time to time."

"So you saw me leave the Vatican?"

"On many occasions. I watched you on many occasions."

"The disguise?"

"At first it fooled me. But then I thought about how almost every day I am seeing a man with funny red hair and a not in fashion suit coming out of the Vatican City. It doesn't fit and I follow you and I know you."

"How much gold do you require to release me?"

"Gold!" Štrekel cried, shooting to his feet. "I require the red gold of your blood!"

The doctor struck him twice with his open hand and then there was the cloth, hot vapours and rolling back again into churning blackness.

XX

WHEN Torturo regained consciousness he was lying, tied with cord to a steel framed bed, with a piece of ply-wood in place of the mattress. The doctor stood over him, with his shirt off, his broad hairy chest glistening with sweat. A bright but uneasy light flickered overhead. To one side sat a small table laden with metallic instruments, objects with throbbing glints, many of which were obviously not originally intended for medical use: curving, serrated blades, heavy chisels, pincers, scalpels, points of steel bristling from jars,—a display certainly not fashioned to set the helpless victim's mind at ease.

"Oh, you are come to," Dr. Štrekel said. "Excellent, now I can begin."

Torturo felt sick to his stomach. His gaze fastened itself on the ominous table by his bedside.

"Begin?" he murmured.

"Yes;—the recant."

"Recant?"

"I have decided to recant my operations."

"Excuse me?"

"You did not fulfil your obligation for services rendered, so I am going to rescind those services."

The doctor cracked his knuckles and picked up a rather dangerous looking saw from the table. Licking his moustache, he gazed down at his captive's legs. Torturo pressed his chin to his chest and followed the direction of the doctor's eyes. He shuddered. His pants' legs were slit down the middle and his scarred but shapely limbs were secured taut, the naked, olive-coloured skin bright beneath the quivering artificial light. He tried to wriggle, to free himself, but the most he could do was to raise his pelvis a few inches off the bed. The doctor had done an excellent job with his knots.

"Hold still."

"Damn you to hell!"

Dr. Štrekel laughed and placed the saw blade against Torturo's left thigh. The latter could feel the slightly prickly steel.

"God help me," he murmured.

The doctor pulled the blade back and the tines dug through the epidermal tissue of the thigh. Torturo winced. The doctor pushed the saw forward, forcefully, and it dug deep, bursting the thin layer of fat, the tines of steel sinking like countless fangs into the priest's flesh.

"A sweet sensation that, eh?" the doctor laughed, his fine white teeth glittering in the light.

Torturo was silent, merely looking at the other with the utmost contempt. His jaw was set and his tongue pressed vigorously against the roof of his mouth, to keep from biting it, to keep from screaming.

"Oh, don't worry, you'll be singing yet," the doctor snarled and, bracing one arm against the man's bound leg and grasping the saw firmly in the other, set to work with grim enthusiasm.

His arm, the forepart like a raw ham, was strained to the utmost, and his broad mouth, stretched to a wicked grin, glistened with two rows of immaculately white teeth. The serrated blade, as it ripped through Torturo's thigh, gave the sensation of a locomotive screaming over piano strings, contacting the nervy muscle with frenzied violence. Torturo gasped and then involuntarily let out a slight cry. There was a coppery taste in his mouth. His teeth tingled and he ground them together. When he breathed in through his nose the air seemed to carry with it a particular odour, a ghastly perfume reminiscent of an abattoir.

"It hurts, eh Papa?"

"Damn it does!" Torturo gasped. "What is it—What in hell do you want?"

"I want this leg."

The doctor's powerful arm swung forward again. Torturo could distinctly feel each muscular fibre as it was severed and fancied he could hear them snap, with a sound like logs crackling in a fire. He was incredibly dizzy. The room spun. He felt as if he were descending into a blistering chasm where bloodstained birds shrieked, fought for his liver and brutal claws dragged him down. To hell he fancied he was going, riding on waves of dancing fire and, encased in this horrid red hot film, he lapsed away.

"Wake up, Papa," the doctor said and doused his face with water.

Torturo licked at the liquid. "Done," he murmured. "Are . . . Are you done?"

"Done?—Don't joke; I'm just beginning!"

Yes, there was still the bright, uneasy light sizzling above him; the table laden with viperous instruments. There was pain and a mingled desire; a desire for life and vengeance, or mercy and death.

"Mercy!" Torturo murmured in agony.

Laughter.

Dr. Štrekel set to work; wiping away the flowing fluid and with the use of clamps separating the tortured flesh. With a small, delicate saw he laboured over the bone. And every twist of its blade sent forth roars of pain which amplified, making all possible description the scattering of hollow shells. The operator obviously knew how to milk the utmost torment from his task. For Torturo the air was too heavy to breathe; it was hot as fire. Like a drunken man he could not see straight; his vision was in bleary doubles. Hallucinating, he fancied the room was dripping with pink blood. The screams came spontaneously from his swollen throat. He dared not look and so shut his eyes, only to see the revolutions of countless brutish sub-beasts; concoctions sprouting from the core of his suffering. They scrambled, bubbling and ate at his face, devoured his nose amidst gloomy, acidic accents and gnawed away at his cheeks with all the glee of starving imps. He shuddered, wheezed and then lapsed once again into darkness.

He opened his eyes. The doctor was there, as if standing at the end of a long, dimly lit tunnel. He heard Štrekel's voice, unclear, incredibly distant.

"Ah, he still breathes! What a constitution! When he breathes no more I will thoroughly dissect him."

Then there was darkness again; darkness mixed with more boiling, ferocious dreams—nightmares in which he saw himself cleft in two and dragged apart; a spiking black moustache prodding him and poking his pain. He dived and swam in his misery and then groped without success. Through black, leafless forests he slid, the sharp, prodding branches festooned with strips of his own skin and mulched with his boiling flesh.

"I'm still tied; I can't feel my face," he thought; and then he tried to speak.

The taste was dreadful. His cheeks were ablaze; his head seemed to be floating in a halo of ignited gas.

"Kc—Kch—Gkch!"

Like a dying rook; and then he peeled back his eyelids. His entire body throbbed with a dull and terrible pain, which gnawed at him like a tribe of toothless cannibals. The truth slowly crept into his disjointed thoughts.

"Gkchh," he murmured. "Hhhh-kch!"

He tried to lick his lips, but simply felt a smarting twitch of muscle; a sensation that was repeated when he attempted to touch his tongue to the roof of his mouth. His gums ached. He tried to wriggle his fingertips, but could not detect any sensation. He tried to wiggle his toes, but his brain failed to find any such appendages. Torturo was in a state of depressed alarm.

226

He was alive, but he had no joy for life. It was a simple syllogism, and the doctor had clearly stated his mode of revenge. The patient, Xaverio Torturo, Pope Lando the Second, had been raped of not only his limbs, but his tongue as well,—at least the tongue that he had been so successfully using. The majority of the teeth of his bottom jaw had been knocked out in the doctor's impetuous struggle to uproot that organ of speech. Torturo's face was butchered. He resembled maggot as much as man.

"And why am I not dead?" he thought. "Why did Dr. Štrekel not kill me?"

Of course the answer came to him quickly enough: The doctor wanted him to feel his own degradation. There would be no use going to so much trouble if he was not able to savour Torturo's misery. Giving the priest a quick and painless death never so much as occurred to Dr. Jure Štrekel, whose entire career had been spent alternatively moulding and butchering the clay of human flesh.

Torturo, regaining his senses to some degree, realised that he was not tied up at all;—he was simply bereft of tongue and limb and therefore presumed to be harmless. He wriggled the butt of his thighs and felt their throbbing soreness. They were hardly healed, and he knew that a lesser man would surely not have survived such physical privation; such gross systematic shock.

Torturo heard steps in the passage, closed his eyes and feigned unconscious. He heard the doctor come in and then felt the man's hand, his thumb press against his throat, his jugular vein.

"Ah good," the doctor murmured. "The devil is still alive."

Then once more alone. A constant, monotonous throbbing, both within and without. His face felt as if it were being licked with flames and there was no tongue to find relief in gnawing. But he was not yet dead, and he knew that while he had this small bit of strength he should act, because before long it would certainly be too late. He tried to clear his mental facilities and let his breath flow with ease. And he waited, letting the air slowly tickle his ravaged nostrils.

Finally, the sound of footsteps could be heard coming down the passage. The doctor walked in and advanced towards the prostrate torso. He stood over it for some moments and then bent down.

"If he is still alive I might just pull out his internals."

Then there were those jaws catching his neck. The man cried out in alarm, and pulled back, but two incisors were firmly attached. Torturo sunk his teeth, the two canines he still had, deep into the meat, biting more savagely than any mad dog. The doctor writhed, struggled and managed to partially free himself, though not without losing a significant chunk of soft tissue from his neck.

Torturo, well realising that the opportunity before him was unique, mastered every muscle in his body and, like a serpent, arced his spine and jettisoned his body forward, jaws open for revenge. He hit pay-dirt, clamping down on the side of the doctor's naked throat. Štrekel attached his powerful hands to Torturo's torso, trying to wrench himself free. The latter sunk the hard white structures that still lined his top jaw deep into the tough meat of the neck. He could feel the doctor's beard scraping against his cheek and hear the man's curses and screams crash into his right ear. He clamped down harder, pressing with his lower gums till they felt near rupture. The jugular vein was pierced and hot fluid came spurting forth conjoined to the doctor's cries of agony and terror. The blood sprayed over Torturo's face and gurgled up over his lips and chin, the liquid filling his strained mouth, a rich and repugnant taste touching his palate. He coughed, freed himself and rolled back, spitting out blood and gasping for breath. The doctor made a vain, spasmodic attempt at movement and gave vent to a few pulpy, uncertain attempts at speech. A droning in Torturo's ears, stillness, and with eyes still open, Štrekel was dead.

The cripple lay immobile, in a state of slight emotion. Gradually he recovered himself and rose up, onto his buttocks. After looking with hatred at the dim chamber and the corpse, he crawled out the door, along the passage and then, with great difficulty, using his chin as a prop, up the stairs.

The stumps of his limbs ached terribly. They were far from properly healed, and in no condition to be strained.

"This will not do," he thought.

Like a sick, dangerous animal he prowled around the apartment, crawling, squirming. The place was small: a bathroom, bedroom and kitchen. The only furniture in the kitchen was a table, with a Sprite bottle full of wine sitting on one corner, and two chairs. A pot sat on the stove, simmering. The bedroom smelled vile. Soiled garments and rags lay scattered on the floor, which was stained with gore. The bed itself, though it now had a mattress, was without dressing. Pushed against one wall was the little table. The metallic instruments, many of them encrusted with dried blood, were scattered in disarray.

He looked at the scene in disgust. The room carried with it all the harrowing visions of his torture, memories shaken frantic by the galloping horror of true nightmares, which to recall made him faint. Reduced to a worm-like state, traumatised and throbbing in the aftermath of the incident, and with the corpse of his tormentor still warm in the basement, it took all Torturo's courage not to give way to gnawing despair.

The aroma from the pot in the kitchen attracted him. Using his mouth, he turned off the burner. He clasped the pot-handle in his jaws and attempted to lift it to the floor. He was unsuccessful. It fell, and overturned. A pile of beans, a semi-liquidy yellow-brown mound, sat steaming on the floor. He stuck his face in the beans and ate. He was starving and they were delicious. The doctor had seasoned them heavily with salt and garlic. Torturo took several mouthfuls and, after swallowing them each in haste, came up for air. He repeated the process fourteen times, until the beans were gone, and then sought out drink.

The Sprite bottle was on the edge of the table, near one corner. Torturo, by pressing himself up against the table's leg, could mount to the height of his nose. He did so, and with his forehead knocked the bottle to the floor. It was plastic and did not break; it was capped and did not spill. He secured the bottle in his crotch and undid the top with his mouth.

He nursed at the bottle, swallowing mouthful upon mouthful of the rich black liquid, the *teran*, which the doctor, like all Slovenians, prized so highly. The liquid stung his gums and the raw place where his tongue had been, filled his nose with its fruity overtures and then slid away down his throat, taking with it a few grains of his misery.—Though he was reduced, he mused, at least he was not dead.

He crawled into the bathroom. There was a brush and a toilet plunger next to the toilet. Taking the toilet plunger in his jaws, he brought it to the kitchen. One of the shirts from the bedroom he ripped into strips with his jaws. He stuck the stump of his right forearm in the rubber half of the plunger. Using his mouth, and the pressure available between his jaw and shoulder, he managed to fasten the plunger tight with the strips of cloth. The result was a crude limb.

He knocked over one of the chairs and, using the pressure of his buttocks, managed to break off three of the four legs. Using strips of cloth, he secured two legs to the front of each of his thighs—the swollen stumps that remained—and one to his left shoulder and nub of forearm.

With his back arched, he moved about the room. His condition was deplorable, but it was slightly less deplorable than it had been two hours earlier. He had been confined for he knew not how long and felt the need for fresh air—the need to storm the Vatican and reclaim his position.

Without hesitation he made his way to the door, turned the handle with his jaws and squirmed through. The door shut behind him. It was late morning and the streets were alive with people. They passed him by, not so much as turning their heads or bestowing an astonished glance on the reduced creature. This was Rome, the greatest city on earth, which, like New York, London and Paris, has the particular quality of extreme Stoicism. In the grand metropolises of the world it takes more than being a scarified cripple to command attention. City dwellers pride themselves on having seen everything. To be startled is considered a breach of proper conduct. Torturo, now truly a mutant, crawled through the streets of Rome; without a tongue, thus unable to speak a few words; without limbs, thus unable to act as he would. Far from being recognised as the rightful bearer of the triple crown, the Chief and Supreme Pastor of the Universe, Vicar of Christ upon Earth, Primate of Italy and the adjacent islands and Patriarch of the Western Church, Torturo found himself deemed not even worthy of so much as a "good day" or a disdainful stare.

He crawled along, practising his crutch-work, his stumps aching sore. Passing in front of a shop window, he looked over. A hideous face stared out at him; a repugnant being, mouth agape, goggled out from the glass. Torturo flushed with startled contempt at this mocking vision, this reflection of his own self, of what he had become.

Shaking his gaze free from the mesmerising portrait of his own downfall, he moved on. Looking around, he recognised the street. It was the via Morgana. He crawled down it and past the monument of Vittorio Emanuele II, which rose up from his right, a mountain of bronze and stone. From his positioning, nearly at ground level, the two charioteers atop the sides of the semicircular colonnade seemed as if they were about to soar into space, the giant rider in the centre as if he was about to topple down and trample the cripple under his horse's hooves. Torturo recalled the day he had stood up on the same monument, in his disguise, like a king going out to mix with the populace. At that time he had stood easily, haughtily in the most exalted position on earth, and if fate were a fiend, this was surely its vengeance.

Slowly and with great difficulty he traversed the backstreets of Rome, the via della Pace and via della Panico, avoiding the busy Corso Vittorio Emanuele II. He crossed the Ponte Sant'Angelo, Bernini's winged statues which lined the way gazing down on him in an almost mocking manner as they floated effortlessly above the river Tiber, which wound slow and filthy through the city like an ever-present greenish brown snake. Passing the Castel Sant'Angelo, he made his way along the via della Conciliazione, and onto St. Peter's Square, that magnificent masterpiece of architecture by Gian Lorenzo Bernini which, to set foot upon is like stepping into some kind of universal eye, human bodies reduced to insectish insignificance, with minds aglow due to the sphere in which their limbs operate. The colonnade of three hundred Doric columns and countless manneristic statues rose up around him, like the rib cage of a giant skeleton. His wounds, much used, began to sting and suppurate. He looked up at the cathedral before him, St. Peter's, behind which stood the Vatican City, the city which was his by right and law and which he was full-ready to reclaim.

The cripple dragged himself forward, through the centre of the piazza and past the Egyptian obelisk, that splendid upright block of phallic stone, which had once served as a turning post in the chariot races at the ancient Circus of Nero. Foot by foot he made his way to the gate. Two Swiss Guards stood before him, blocking all passage. His heart was glad. He knew them both by name: Betschart and Meier; two young men who had always stood by him in awed deference. Torturo gazed up at them. They did not move. They stood immobile, looking slightly ridiculous in their sixteenth-century style outfits of black, red, and yellow: black hats dangling with red string, legs sheathed in dark-yellow stockings and feet in buckled shoes.

"Ckhhhaaggghh!" Torturo croaked.

Meier, for a brief instant, glanced down, and then returned to his stance of statuesque indifference. The cripple approached Betschart and tried desperately to articulate his name.

"Aeckhhhaagghh," he croaked.

The young man stared straight before him, not so much as flinching. He was obviously well-trained.

Torturo felt his brain boiling. Surely there must be some way for him to make himself known, for him to get inside his fortress and identify his holy presence. If Meier would only recognise him, how richly the young man would be rewarded;—Lando the Second would see to that!

He turned and gazed over St. Peter's Square. Tourists were scattered over it like exotic beetles, their figures, fat, hunched and ill-dressed, looking thoroughly disgusting against the background of idealistic sculptures: finely wrought men and gracefully clad women.—One figure on the square, however, was not that of a tourist. Plump and sheathed in ecclesiastic garments, it made its way towards the entrance with short, rapid steps. There was no mistaking the man: It was Di Quaglio.

"Ah, he will surely recognise me!" thought Torturo with a sudden thrill of hope. "He was always a loyalist."

Di Quaglio approached the scene, but did not so much as turn his gaze toward the cripple.

"Aeckh," Torturo belched. "Aeckhhhaagghh!"

Di Quaglio looked down at him with undisguised disgust.

"What is this?" he asked Meier.

"A beggar, sir," Meier answered stiffly.

"Well, see that he is removed. It hardly gives a desirable impression to have his sort lingering out front."

Di Quaglio entered the Vatican City and made his way to his own offices. Since the disappearances, of Vivan, Zuccarelli and then the very Pope himself, an enormous burden of responsibility had fallen on the shoulders of the plump little cardinal. His desk was piled high with papers, innumerable documents to sign, countless requests, policies to consider and questions of grave importance to be dealt with.

He sighed as he looked at the mess before him. Aside from letters, a number of parcels sat off to one side to be opened. He decided to deal with these first, as their bulk seemed of greater interest than the minutia of documents.

One package was larger than the rest. It was a good-sized cardboard box, with the return address being of a certain convent on the outskirts of Rome. The cardinal tore away the tape, ripped at the cardboard and looked within. It contained two arms, two legs and a tongue in a plastic bag. On the ring finger of the right hand of the right arm was the fisherman's ring. Though the package had been posted some days earlier, and the contents were most likely a good deal older than that, there was no unpleasant odour or signs of decay.

Di Quaglio was horrified. He immediately telephoned the Prefect of the Papal Household.

"The Pope is dead!" he cried. "Lando the Second is no more!"

The Prefect of the Papal Household informed the Camerlengo who, in the presence of the Papal Master of Ceremonies, the cleric prelates of the Apostolic Camera, and the Secretary of the Apostolic Camera verified that the limbs did indeed appear to be those of Lando the Second. The Camerlengo, according to tradition, called out the name of the Pope three times. The limbs lay still; the tongue did not respond. The secretary of the Apostolic Camera drew up the death certificate. The Camerlengo then informed the Vicar of Rome. The vicar, through an address over the Vatican radio, informed the people of Rome and the world.

Meanwhile the prefect of the papal household met with the dean of the college of cardinals who informed the rest of the college, the ambassadors accredited to the Holy See, the presidents of Italy and the United States, as well as the Prime Minister of England.

The Camerlengo had all the property of Lando the Second removed from the Sistine Chapel and locked and sealed in private chambers. A will was looked for, but none was found. The Pope's fisherman's ring and his seal were broken to prevent forgeries. Arrangements were made for the papal funeral rights, and the nine days of mourning begun. The reign of Lando the Second was at an end.

On October 21st of the same year he was canonised a saint. His limbs and tongue, after being bathed in rapeseed oil, were removed to the Santa Maria Maggiore and placed in windowed golden caskets in the Cappella Paolina, on display for all the pious to see. The oil, oleum martyr, was divided into ten thousand flasks inscribed with the words *Eulogia Tou Agiou Lando*. These were distributed to the faithful as a remedy against sickness.

XXI

THE cripple watched Di Quaglio disappear inside the Vatican City and then felt the hands of the two Swiss Guards, Betschart and Meier, take him up and deposit him some distance away. He felt sickened with helplessness. One thing was obvious: he needed to get out of Rome. In his present condition, survival was too difficult in the city. He could hardly hope to ever gain admittance into the Vatican, and even if he were to, who would recognise him, or want to? He knew of only one person in the world whom he could fully trust, and that was his cousin. His cousin was in Padua. Torturo could not call him, because he could not speak. He could not write, as he had not hands to write with.

Slowly he crawled along, over the Tiber, along the via Cavour. He made his way through the Piazza Vittorio Emanuele II, through the knots of ostentatious whores that were already there even though it was just past two in the afternoon, and then crossed the via Giovanni Giolitti, to the train station. As usual it was busy, filled with pimps, pickpockets garbed as respectable citizens, businessmen and slovenly dressed tourists.

Torturo looked at the board. There was a train departing for Milan, via Florence, in a quarter of an hour. From Milan, Padua was but a few hours journey. He had no money for a ticket and cursed his own stupidity for having neglected to secure the doctor's wallet.—Still, as often as not the train attendants never even bothered to ask one for a ticket. It was undoubtedly an easy enough matter to attain one's destination without money.—And, in any case, he had little choice but to try. It was apparent that Rome offered him very little hospitality.

Working his way through the multitude of travellers, he crawled to the track designated on the board. He clambered up the steps and onto the train. No one offered him help and, with nothing to facilitate communication but a mouth full of croaking pain, he could ask for none. The train itself was full and no seats were available for those without reservations. People filled the aisles and even stood in the luggage section and in front of the restrooms—the section which was for Torturo most convenient to access.

"With the train so crowded, they will most likely neglect asking for tickets," he thought.

It was true that people stared at him, but the train nonetheless pulled out of the station without anyone questioning him. Soon he saw the grey sky flashing by through the windows and felt the tracks bouncing beneath him. The train, which was an intercity, began to make its stops, each one accompanied by a staticky announcement made over the speakers: *Stimigliano, Orte, Attigliano.*

239

As he sat in the corner, the evil smell of the latrine assailing his nose, his mind wandered back to that first lone train ride, when he was still a boy. He remembered saying goodbye to his cousin and uncle and how he afterwards took up his old-fashioned grip and boarded the iron beast. How exultant, how high-spirited he had been, flying over rivers and past lakes, with the snow-capped blue mountains behind them, and the words and teachings of Father Falzon as a foundation to live by.

Now he felt the throbbing pain of his tortured body and inhaled the stench of the toilet. Few beings had seen such highs and lows, experienced a stroke so severe. It was as bad as the hanging of Nuncomar; it was comparable to the downfall of Richard II. Huddled in his corner, sneered at by every being that passed him by, he suffered like an eagle fallen into a pit.

When the train pulled out of Montevarchi, he felt some relief. He was almost as far as Florence, which was halfway to Milan. From Milan he would make his way to Padua, where his cousin was installed in the role of bishop. Mentally and physically exhausted, he closed his eyes and tried to think of better things.

"You have a ticket?"

He felt something prodding him and looked. A man was nudging him with his boot; another looming menacingly behind him.

"A ticket? You have a ticket?"

He was silent.

"Ticket? Where is your ticket?"

He opened his mouth and croaked, the sound deep, resonant and disturbing.

"*Basta!*" the man cried. "Luigi! Give me a hand. This cripple doesn't have a ticket!"

"Disgusting fellow—But damn he's heavy!"

Torturo, the cripple, was hurled off the train as it pulled into Florence, his wooden apertures clattering against the stone platform. He looked up. A number of people were staring at him (overfed Northerners, their bellies protruding; solemn Florentines who gazed at him as if he were less than nothing). Others, in a rush, stepped hastily over him, almost on him. Cursing internally, he rallied himself and made his way through the station, to the exit. Outside it was raining: a fall rain, humid and heavy that left the streets deserted of pedestrians; the streets rushed with bubbling fluid that gathered swirling at the gutters. He stared out through the glass window, oppressed and undecided in what course to take.

"There is no loitering in here."

This time it was a policeman—a young, fascist looking fellow with a closely trimmed beard and dispassionate black eyes.

"There is no loitering in here," in a curt, authoritative voice. And then, opening the door and ushering the cripple outside: "Move on; the rain will clear up soon if you are lucky."

Torturo obeyed, hobbling, crawling forward on his sticks, into the downpour. The liquid ran over his head, into his eyes, and down the back of his neck. It seemed that there was a certain breed of man who asked nothing better than to be able to push around, to harry weaker beings, revenge their stupidity on those without fists to fight.—The cripple spit into the rain. The bells of the city rang gloomily through the wet sky, tolling the hour of six. He was not lucky; the rain, instead of abating, increased dramatically in strength. By the time he had found shelter beneath an alcove, he was soaked through. He looked up at the grey, impenetrable heavens overhead and running street before him, heard his own stomach moaning with hunger and drank hard from misery's cup. In these moments alone, stripped of more than his grandeur and title, stripped of his very limbs and features, his very tongue with which to articulate, the thoughts came—not with rapidity or precision, but as a haunting nightmare. His recollections and feelings were black, and more painful than any festering wound. He thought of his mentor, Father Falzon, and wondered whether the man were in heaven or hell, reborn as scavenging dog or roving demi-god. He had always considered himself to be in some way the avenger of that man's neglected life; but from where he now grovelled, in the state of a limbless, creeping creature, he knew that his ambitions had miscarried and he was but little more than a despicable abortion. He recalled his own youth, spent in wicked trivialities and the pursuit of arcane knowledge. He had climbed to the top of the pinnacle of the Church and had fallen—fallen with shattering briskness, in a horrible, lightening-like flash. To have toppled from such a staggering height was devastating. His life was blasted; he did not repent; yet he was sorely disappointed. He thought of those whom he had healed and considered the irony of his situation. Others he had healed, but now had not the power to heal himself.

That night he spent without a roof over his head and without food in his belly, crawling around the wet city of Florence. He passed the sham house of Dante, and tasted hell on his palate. He crawled along the via dei Calzaiuoli to the Piazza della Signora and saw the sculptures, those reproductions of Donatello and Michelangelo and the incomparable original of Cellini, mock him with their grandeur while a policeman eyed him with suspicion. Scurrying off, he found himself on the banks of the Arno. He crawled under the Ponte San Niccolo in the hope of finding there a dry place to sleep, but a group of young men were there drinking beer and smoking marijuana. They laughed, made obscene, cruel jokes and threw bottles at him. He fled and disappeared into the night like a wounded dog. He had no blanket but the late October drizzle.

The next morning he crawled through the central market, crowded with people and food on all sides: breads, cheeses, green and black olives, stacks of plums, apples and pears, prosciutto crudo and cooked ham, almonds, cashews, raisins and dates. The butchers sat behind counters well stocked with pink rabbits, joints of beef and pork and mounds of raw and roasted chickens, while the fish sellers dived their fists into barrels of muscles and oysters, trays of squids, prawns and fresh sardines glistening on all sides. At Nerbone, the famous market kitchen, the cripple saw workers sit down with great bowls of chick-pea soup, plates of macaroni and

243

pitchers of the cheap but delicious house wine. He was starved and the sights and aromas made him feel faint. A woman, seeing his hungry eyes and thinking him a beggar, threw him a roll. It was warm and delicious and he ate it, in desperate haste, like a savage.

His existence was degraded, and he spent his days scrounging. Humbled by hunger, he felt as if he had a yoke of iron around his neck. He begged in front of the Santa Maria del Fiore. The tourists, ever ready to spend ten euros on a museum, one hundred on a restaurant meal, or a two hundred on a hotel room, simply could not find it in their hearts to bestow a few coins on the cripple. His appearance disgusted people and they chose to stay as far away from him as possible, lest they catch whatever it was he had. Thus, for him, to even find basic sustenance seemed impossible.

He was lucky to get a piece of bread or an old bit of vegetable. Meat never crossed his lips. In dire need of nutrition, warmth and care, he had only hunger, the open sky and the yellow spit of obnoxious young men. After weeks of this, of begging, of sleeping on any dry patch he could manage to appropriate for an hour, he looked at the drizzling heavens, thought on God and considered his cruel divinity. Presently the rain stopped and he crawled along the sober cold bricks, his head spinning, filled with the pangs and darkness of sorrow. Crucified by sheer bodily weakness, he collapsed and let his eyes close against that chilly surface which had once been baked by fire.

Two figures approached him, their heads covered with black hoods, which had round holes cut out for the eyes, and their bodies draped with black robes of coarse cloth. They inspected the cripple, lying before them as one dead, a stinking heap of debased humanity, murmured to each other, and then hoisted him on their shoulders and carried him away. A quarter of an hour later he was set down in front of the outer precinct of the Sette Santi convent.

A nun bent over him and pressed a glass of water coloured with wine to his lips. He sucked at the liquid and swallowed gratefully.

"The brothers of the Confraternita della Misericordia placed you here," she said. "They asked us to see that you are fed."

Apparently she read the questioning gaze in his eyes, for she continued: "They are a particular order, their members come from all stations of life. Many are rich and aristocratic, while others are simply artisans. They take it as their sworn duty to help the miserable and destitute. You must be thankful for their attention."

Torturo was thankful. He was starving, and the nuns gave him bread and soup. Though they were unable to offer him lodging beyond that necessary in order to bring him out of immediate danger, they procured him sleeping tickets for one of the local hostels. He was allowed a bed from eight every night until six in the morning. The sisters told him that for as long as he pleased he could return to Sette Santi every afternoon for their charity lunch, which he did.

One young nun, Sister Justina, who had particularly gentle manners, took it upon herself to feed the wretch. Her face was round and her figure slight and, though she was not by any means handsome, her quiet voice was full of warmth and her gaze radiant with compassion. When she could, she took him to a private place and washed him; she scrubbed his torso with a stiff sponge and lathered his scanty hair, wilfully overcoming her disgust. She pitied him, for he was the most appalling man she had ever seen, and wished she could do more to relieve his suffering. His eyes were strong and intelligent, and she could not help but believe his thoughts were in like accord. Occasionally, after the meal, she read to him for a quarter of an hour from the Holy Bible. He blinked and sighed in obvious appreciation. She was pleased that he responded to the teachings of Jesus Christ and was sorrowful that her time and position forbade her from further charity.

"Might I not read to him for five more minutes?" she would ask the abbess, Mother Barbara, when called away.

"I am afraid not," was the recurring answer. "It is admirable that you find joy in such charitable endeavours, but forming a particular attachment to a needy individual is not to be borne. Your attention must be turned towards your other duties, for you are more than just this solitary cripple's helpmate. It is obviously the Lord's will that he suffer so—undoubtedly for some unspeakable sin;—The proper course for you, my dear, is not to do more than you are asked . . . In any case, the gout in my feet is especially bad right now, and your spare moments should rightly be spent massaging them."

Sister Justina was Mother Barbara's favourite. The latter enjoyed her, guarded her with a jealous eye and never tired of having the young woman's small, soft hands running over her own sore joints. Though Justina did not take pleasure in the hungry passion of the abbess, she tolerated it, such being the ways of the convent.

One day, after feeding the cripple his soup and reading him an excerpt from *The Gospel According to Mark*, Sister Justina gave him a gift. He had been particularly solemn and thoughtful that day, and she thought her surprise might cheer him up.

"It is a nice wool cap," she said, putting it on his head. "I made it—to keep you warm up top."

He looked at her sadly.

"Don't you like it?"

He nodded his head.

"You do?"

He nodded his head. "Yes."

He moved slowly through the old, open hallway, towards the exit, the new cap, which was a sky blue, bright on his head. The nun walked by his side, chattering lightly as she went. They came to the door and she opened it.

"*Ciao*," she said smiling. "See you tomorrow."

The cripple shook his head.

"I will not see you tomorrow?"

The cripple shook his head. "No."

"You have something to do tomorrow? Then I will see you the next day?"

He shook his head.

"Not then either?"

"No."

"Well, when *will* I see you?"

He looked at her gravely, almost sternly.

"Won't you come back? Won't I see you again?"

He shook his head. "No."

"You will leave Florence?"

He nodded, his eyes still stern and penetrating.

"You are going on a voyage?" she asked with concern.

The cripple nodded his head. "Yes."

The bells of the city began to strike three o'clock, their tintinnabulation echoing out sonorous, petulant, demanding.

"It is the time when I must attend Mother Barbara," the nun said. "But wait here, let me get you something before you go."

Before the cripple could respond, she was dashing away, her habit fluttering around her ankles and collecting around her young figure. In less than ten minutes she returned, carrying a purse in which were two loaves of bread, some olives, a hunk of Parmesan cheese and a twenty euro note.

She kneeled down and hung the purse around his neck.

"This is for your trip," she said. "Some food for your trip," she blushed. "And a little money,—It is almost nothing, but it might help."

He looked at her: firmly, sorrowfully.

Just then Mother Barbara appeared, her stout figure filling the passage behind them. Her tremendous, sensual second chin hung palpitating with emotion and the black hair on her pale upper lip stood out with frightening clarity.

"Come girl!" she cried. "Enough dawdling with that cursed cripple. It is the time for you to massage my feet. I have been walking on them all day, involved in

248

labour upon labour, and they are in sore need of your caresses. Come—Hurry, before you put me completely out of temper!"

"I have to go," the nun said sadly. Then, when Mother Barbara's back was turned, the young woman quickly kissed Torturo on the forehead, got up and darted off, with a broken goodbye, one hand straying to her eyes as she retreated.

"Goodbye," he thought, as he turned and crawled away.

He made his way along the Lungamo Generale Diaz. The shops were just beginning to open. The weather was overcast and streets damp, but it was not raining. He crawled along the Loggiato degli Uffizi, past the gallery, past the busts of Dante, Leonardo da Vinci and Galileo. At the Piazza della Signora, in front of Bandinello's *Hercules*, looking more like a sack of melons leaning against a wall than a demi-god, a crowd of Japanese tourists parted for him, with comments of joint interest and disgust. A number took pictures of the twisted chopped up monster, the sub-beast, thinking him about as interesting as anything they had yet seen in Florence.

He crawled past the Church of San Michele, past Verrocchio's *Incredulity of St. Thomas*, a bronze masterpiece of Christ urging the sceptical apostle to shove his hand in his pierced side. Pleasure seekers were just starting to appear along the street, taking advantage of the break in the weather, eager to search out a glass of wine or a cappuccino and to be amongst people; the people who were, for Torturo, no more than ghosts.

XXII

OVER the months the nubs of his shoulders and butts of his thighs, all that remained of his limbs, had grown especially strong, taking up as they were the entire burden of his person in all its shifting about. When he set off on the road from town he moved slowly, but much less slowly than might be expected from one in his condition, without either arms or legs. He made his way along the narrow strip of gravel and dirt that sat between the road and the ditch to one side, moving steady and resolute, despite the never-ending stream of traffic that roared by him. Cars sounded their horns, trucks and buses splashed him with mud. The day wore away in this monotonous struggle for distance, darkness fell and he was forced to crawl completely off the road, to avoid being run over. He travelled the fields, his crutches sinking in the mud, his body often getting caught up in barbed-wire fences, dogs occasionally coming upon him, barking and trying to make a meal of his burly stumps. He fought them off, roaring inarticulately, jabbing with his stalks of wood.

By the time he reached the village of Vaglia it was half-past two in the morning and he was thoroughly spent. Using his jaws as a tool, he worked a hunk of bread from his pouch. He swallowed a few mouthfuls, washing it down with water sipped from a puddle and then fell asleep in a stand of weeds. The next morning he was awoken by a slug crawling across his face. He shouldered it away, rinsed his face in the puddle, relieved himself in the weeds, and resumed his northward journey.

The second day was harder than the first. The sky was dark with clouds and, at nine in the morning, began to scatter fresh rain, which gradually increased in strength into a downpour that lasted throughout the day. The cripple crawled along the gravel, through the mud, wet and dismal. When he passed through villages people stared at him in amazement. No one had ever seen such a down-trodden creature. He was like a leper from another age and people felt an instinctive inclination to avoid him as if he were a sack of diseased flesh. He travelled through Ponte Ghieretto, over the Passo della Futa, through Firenzuola and Pietramala, and after exhausting himself on the Passo della Raticosa, fell asleep beneath a pine tree, the rain still falling with vigour. Awaking in the middle of the night, he shivered with the first phases of influenza. As hearty as his constitution was, it was being taxed to the extreme. Not able to fall back asleep, he vomited and then crawled towards the road. The rain had stopped, but the moonless sky was black. Tremors shook his body as he crawled; the wood strapped to his thighs scraped along the asphalt.

Though the traffic was extremely light, every car that passed him nearly ran him over. With thoughts unclear he began to hallucinate, fancying he saw the roadway marked with pools of blood and the majestic pines that shot up from the hillsides as never-ending crucifixion scenes. The earth swung beneath him. He himself was a monstrous toad, bloated with wriggling worms of flame which scrambled for escape through the orifices of his head.—And he prayed. In a continuous moan he said prayers for some simple time without horror and pain.

When daylight came, grey and mournful, his feverish state somewhat subsided. He ate a mouthful of Parmesan cheese, rallied himself, and continued forward. Though he knew he was ill, he did his best not to slacken his pace. Light blended into darkness and reality was infused with faint hallucinations, halls hung with skins and familiar joints, the seemingly endless roadway scattered with sharp thorns. There was blackness and an occasional hour of sleep procured in some dry patch of ground, beneath a tree or hedge, occasionally in an old barn. Then there was again aching and travel and fever. The clouds blew in over the hills and seemed puffed full of wrath. In the distance there were scars of yellow light. The storm was electric. Wind and rain shook through the branches of the trees, screamed in the air, and, attacking in horizontal sheets, flailed his tortured body, as if wanting to pound the very life out of him. He could scarcely breathe. The rain pricked like needles. Wet to the kidneys, his nose ran with mucous and throat swelled with pain. He collapsed, his face sunk in the mud. He felt as if he could not move another inch, but, with a supreme effort of will, he propped himself on his crutches and moved another mile.

At dawn the weather broke. The countryside shone, glossy green. Half dead, he climbed over a hill. Down below he saw the city of Padua, in the midst of which glittered the seven cupolas of the Basilica del Santo. Travelling on average nineteen hours a day, the entire journey had taken him twenty-three days.

XXIII

AT the base of the steps, a being struggled. About knee-high, with wooden crutches strapped on in place of his four limbs, like an image by Breughel, the man was trying desperately to mount the steps. The people around him stood back a respectable distance, though more from fear than the desire to accommodate. With beggarly rags hanging about him, and an unearthly stench rising, permeating his vicinity, this glob of human suffering was truly grotesque. His features were swollen and indistinguishable. A woollen cap, which sat perched atop his skull, fell off as he struggled, revealing a glossy red scalp with thick, wiry hairs clinging to it. The man swivelled his neck and looked back imploringly.

"Ewww!" a young woman said, upon seeing his face.

But, in every group of cowards there are inevitably a few heroes. Two stout men, young, generous and beef-fed, ran up from the back of the line.

"Yes, good, help the poor fellow up the steps," a woman said.

One perched the cap on the glossy scalp and then together they heaved the limbless being up by the armpits and ascended the steps, the queue moving aside for them with murmurs of admiration for their effort and a mixture of contempt and pity for their burden.

"*Ecco*," one of the men said as they shoved their burden up against the glass case.

The tongue, red and ripe as a strawberry, sat enclosed within, resting atop a gold pin and highlighted against a background of gold brocade. Torturo felt the stump of his own organ, bereft of branch, unable to speak or even properly taste, quiver at the back of his throat. A croak, hoarse and awful, escaped his distended lips.

"He is telling us to let him down."

"That's fine. He has looked long enough."

"Ckhhhaaggghh!" Torturo croaked.

"*Prego, prego*," the men said, hoisting him back down the stairs and setting him on the floor.

The cripple moaned, inarticulate and frightful. His bottom jaw was nearly toothless and those on the top glistened like fangs in the maw of some blood-thirsty animal. His eyes flashed scorn. He turned and, with the utmost difficulty, made his way from the chapel, his crutches clicking and scraping against the marble floor.

Outside the weather was cool but clear. He pushed himself up against the wall near the church entrance. He gazed up at the great equestrian statue to his right, *The Gattamelata* of Donatello, and his wool cap fell off again. The cripple buried his chin in his chest and thought of her who had given him the gift; he felt the difficulty of loss. Through half-open, slightly moist eyes he stared at the woven, blue, soft hair of sheep. He was weak with hunger and fatigue and nearly drowned in disappointment. A coloured slip of paper came down. A five-euro note floated into his cap. He glanced up.

"Kgau!" he croaked.

There were those features, soft and gentle, glowing above him; the garments ecclesiastic; the entire figure familiar.

"Ehhgg! Mmmmmmaaaa!"

"Pardon?"

"Mmmmmmaaaa!"

"Is that not enough? You want more you say?" Marco asked, raising his eyebrows. "Well, here poor fellow, here is another five;—and may God bless you."

"Ehhgg! Ckhhhaaggghh!"

"*Prego, prego.*"

"Mmmmmmaaaa! Mmmmmmaaaaarrr!"

"What is it he is trying to tell me? He is quite exasperated!"

"Mmmmmmaaaa! Ehhgghhhaaggghh. Mmmmmmaaaaarrrkgha—kgha—kgha."

"Why, it sounds like he is trying to pronounce my name!" Marco said with astonishment. "Are you trying to say Marco?"

The cripple nodded his head, his eyes glowing with excitement.

"Do you know me?"

Again, he nodded his head.

Marco kneeled down near him and looked closely at his dismantled features and then eyes. He was silent. He bit his bottom lip.

"Mmmmmmaaaarrrkgha—kghau."

"My God!"

"Mmmmaaarrkghau!" the cripple cried, opening his hideous mouth wide.

"Your eyes!"

"Mmarrkghau!"

Marco looked aghast. "Cousin!" he murmured.

Marco did not know how it was that this devastated cripple was the same man, the same Xaverio Torturo, who he had grown up with, the same Lando the Second who was the rightful Pope, but he knew it was so. Marco's was a sensitive nature. Though he did not recognise the body before him, he recognised the soul that spoke from behind that pair of harrowed, suffering, and yet unbeaten eyes.

He brought the cripple back to his chambers, where he fed him with hot broth, wine and water. He bathed him, scrubbing his body with a stiff sponge and lathering it with a pleasant smelling avocado soap. Afterwards he shaved the wiry tangles of hair from Torturo's chin and upper lip and clipped short the straggling hairs on his head.

"Now, here, lie down in my bed. You need some rest."

He hoisted the cripple atop the soft mattress and tucked him in. Torturo, submerged in a mass of clean sheets and blankets, let out a sigh and closed his eyes. Within seconds he was fast asleep.

✻

"Ahh, there you are," Marco said gently, when he saw his cousin emerge from the bedroom nearly thirty-six hours later. "You look much better now. How do you feel?"

Torturo nodded his head and gave his cousin a grateful look.

"Now, what else do you need?"

"Ckhhheeggghh; ckhheeggghhaur."

"What is it you want?"

"Ckhheeggghhaur."

Marco divined. "You want a cigarette?" said he.

Torturo nodded.

"Yes, you always were a great smoker. Wait here—I will go buy you a pack of Parisiennes.—That is your brand."

In the days that followed Torturo's health improved. Though he was still far from robust, he seemed to be out of immediate danger. Marco cared for him with true affection, feeding and dressing him with his own hands and, at the breakfast table, turning the pages of the newspaper for Torturo to read. Marco's was a compassionate nature, and he wanted his cousin to prosper.

"Well, one thing is certain," said Marco, "we must prove to the world who you are and install you once again in your rightful place as the Vicar of Christ upon Earth. Since you were declared dead a new conclave has taken place. Gonzales got his way. They elected Hojeda. He took the name of Pope Clement the Fifteenth. But of course he is not anything of the sort. You are the Pope, not him. We must prove to the world who you are!"

Torturo smiled sourly. He shook his head, "No."

"You don't think we would be able to prove your case?"

Torturo looked at him gravely.

"Do you not want to be Pope?"

The cripple did not stir.

Marco repeated the question: "Do you want to be Pope, the Vicar of Christ upon earth?"

Torturo shook his head, "No."

It was one of the first days of spring. Marco wheeled his cousin through the Orto Botanico, the botanical gardens of Padua, which, dating back to 1545, is one of the oldest botanical gardens in the world. They went over the beautiful walks, which were just beginning to burst with greenery and scented flowers. Marco talked little, only now and again reading the names and histories of the various plants. They stopped beneath the shade of the beautiful magnolias which, dating from the 1700s, are the oldest in Europe. Afterwards, they saw the four-hundred-year-old Göethe palm, by which the famous German poet formed his theory of evolution. There were beautiful creepers, succulents, a greenhouse full of orchids and ferns, and a pond carpeted with water lilies and other aquatic plants. Torturo gazed fondly over the poisonous plant garden, the *Veratrum nigrum* and *Aconitum napellus*, the *Gelsemium*, or false jasmine, with its lanceolate leaves and its gorgeous and fragrant funnel-shaped flowers. In the three rooms of the orangery, aside from philodendron, Japanese pepper and scented pelargonium, numerous carnivorous plants sat with open maws: cobra lilies, *Nepenthes* with their coiling tentacles and the staghorn sundew, with its giant twenty-three-inch leaves.

The air was heavy with perfume. The cripple breathed in deeply through his nostrils and then smiled sadly.

"Beautiful, isn't it?" Marco said.

Torturo nodded his head, "Yes."

There was a pause. Marco felt deeply for his cousin. The man, just months before, had been in the highest position in the Catholic world; he had been incredibly fit, charismatic, and energetic. It had seemed as if his destiny was to do great things. But here he was now, a croaking, obscure cripple, raped of the powers to properly function, with eyes growing dim of exultation. If he lacked the will to live it was no wonder.

"Would you like a cigarette?"

"Yes."

Marco took the pack from Torturo's pocket, knocked one out and stuck it in the latter's mouth. Torturo took a long drag, held it momentarily in his lungs and then exhaled through his nose, the grey plume rising up and slowly melting into the sky.

"I need to buy some panbiscotto and cheese," Marco said. "Shall we go to the shop now?"

Torturo agreed and the two men leisurely made their way out of the garden, the cripple wheeled along, gazing at the plants and blooms around him with a sort of sad satisfaction. While going along the Vicolo Santonini, a youngish priest, probably in his late twenties, overtook them.

"Ah, Father Massimo!" Marco cried. "How do you do?"

"Very well, thank you. I am out for my afternoon constitutional. And how are you?" (He looked down at Torturo and smiled pityingly.) "How are you and your friend?"

Torturo nodded.

"Very well, thank you," Marco replied. "Simply out enjoying this beautiful spring weather. Please join us."

The two priests and the cripple moved along, the former engaged in pleasant conversation, the latter slowly puffing at the cigarette which dangled from his lips. The young priest was lively and his bright, handsome face shone as he talked, telling the bishop a humorous anecdote concerning Dante, the Seventh Circle of Hell, and the father of Enrico Scrovegni. Gradually the three men came to the Ponte Molino and, crossing it, stopped half-way. The sun struck them in full and the Bachiglione River ran beneath, a beautiful gurgling brownish green. Father Massimo continued to talk. The cripple surveyed the surrounding area, the spinning river and its banks, an old woman hanging clothes out to dry from her window, a boy by the water's edge playing with a dog.

"*Un piccolo piccolo Lassie, un pic-co-lo Lassie!*" the boy sang.

Though neither of the two men, standing and conversing, took any notice of the boy, Torturo's eyes were firmly set in that direction. While singing, the boy tied a large stone to the end of the leash.

Marco touched his own head with the palm of his hand. "Ah, I forgot!" he exclaimed. "I still need to buy the groceries. Do you mind watching my friend while I run quickly into the shop?"

"Certainly not," Father Massimo replied. "I would be delighted to stay here with him."

Marco ran across the street. The young priest, leaning with his back against the parapet of the bridge and humming to himself, stayed with Torturo.

Torturo watched as the boy picked up the dog.

"*Un piccolo piccolo Lassie, un pic-co-lo Lassie!*" the boy sang, and then lifting the dog over his head, flung it into the river. "*Un piccolo piccolo Lassie, un pic-co-lo Lassie!*" The boy stood on the bank of the river dancing and laughing. The dog struggled briefly and then, pulled down by the weight of the rock, sank.

The young priest had turned and witnessed the finale of this cruel act. In a flash, he threw off his cassock, revealing a well-fashioned, masculine body, jumped upon the parapet of the bridge and dived off. The water at this part of the river was deceptive. It looked tolerably deep, but was not. Sharp rocks lurked beneath the dark green water. Father Massimo plowed heavily into the river, struck his head against such a rock and rolled into the water. The boy screamed. A few pedestrians had seen the priest jump. They gathered at the edge of the bridge, but none ventured into the river in which the young ecclesiastic was sinking, unconscious. The people discussed the matter, almost calmly, while the minutes passed.

Finally, a gaunt gentleman in a leisure suit approached and, upon being informed what the problem was, proceeded to take action. He peeled off his jacket and shirt and slid off the bank, into the water. With great effort he recovered the body and brought it to shore, just as Marco was returning, carrying a bag of groceries. Torturo's cousin, who was the Bishop of Padua, gave a cry of alarm when he saw the body laid out on the grassy bank of the Bachiglione. Throwing the groceries to one side, he hurried across the bridge and down to the shaded bank. The face and lips of Father Massimo were white and he did not breathe. Presently a doctor appeared on the scene. He examined the priest minutely and attempted mouth-to-mouth resuscitation, followed by the Heimlich manoeuvre.

"How is he?" Marco asked anxiously, seeing the exasperated expression on the doctor's face.

"He's dead," the man said. "He has drowned."

"By God, he is dead!" someone in the gathering crowd shouted.

Marco ran a finger over the young man's cheek.

"Yes," he said. "His soul has flown to heaven."

The body trembled slightly.

"He is trembling," Marco observed.

"So he is," the doctor said. "It is a muscle spasm I suppose. Not uncommon."

Marco looked at the trembling corpse and held his breath.

Of a sudden, a rippling, snake-like surge ran through the young priest's body. He quaked violently; his left arm lashed the ground; his head whipped forward and he coughed, his tongue lunging from his mouth. After spitting out a mouthful of bilious fluid, Father Massimo sat up with eyes wide and bloodshot.

Marco's heart danced in his breast. "He's alive," he murmured. "He has returned to the land of the living!"

"I . . . I must have been mistaken," the doctor mumbled. "Sometimes the vital signs are impossible to perceive."

The young priest smiled awkwardly and gasped for air. His skin was still ashen white. An ambulance appeared on the scene and he was rushed off to the hospital amidst the applause of the onlookers.

"Ah, cousin Torturo!" Marco said to himself as the ambulance sped away. He turned and walked quickly back over the bridge, where the cripple had been left unattended for the past half hour.

The creature was there, slumped in his wheelchair, chin pressed against chest.

"He has nodded off to sleep."

Marco gathered up the groceries which he had cast aside and sat them on the lap of the cripple. Only then did he notice the parted lips and pallid stillness.

"Cousin?"

He took hold of a shoulder and shook it.

"Cousin!"

He bent over and stared at the ravaged, torment-tempered face. The cripple breathed no more. Tears filled the Bishop of Padua's eyes, rolled down his cheeks and fell on his cousin's neck;—the neck of one who had suffered much and had fallen from the staggering heights of glory. Xaverio Torturo was dead; he had died in the spring sun, his body wasted.

XXIV

MARCO sat in his office, the same which had once belonged to Bishop Vivan, his gentle features infused with an infinite sadness. He mulled over paperwork, occasionally taking a sip from a glass of ginger ale which was by his side. His cousin was dead, and he mourned. He had had the body cremated and, just that morning, scattered the ashes in the Bachiglione River. He considered this to be more noble than a grave which could never be marked.

What sorrowed him most, however, was not so much the death, but the mystery of the departed soul. In the state that Torturo had been, death was an alternative not to be altogether despised—That is, if his soul managed to escape eternal perdition. On this score, however, Marco was far from certain. He had no exact knowledge of Torturo's relationship with the Supreme Being, but feared it was not all that it should have been. That he, Marco, was a grievous sinner, he well knew. He must repent, and struggle for cleanliness of life, purify himself by fulfilling his duties in a seamless manner. But his cousin? Had Torturo had time to clear up any uncertainties regarding his own destiny prior to death?

Presently there was a knock at the door.

"*Avanti*," Marco called out despondently.

Father Massimo walked in, a wide grin upon his face.

"I am glad to see you are up and about," Marco said seriously, rising from his chair. "You gave us a terrible fright the other day."

"But there was a death," the other laughed.

"Yes." Marco found the laugh positively disgusting. "My friend . . . My friend was unfortunate."

"It is strange, is it not?"

"Strange?"

"That he died;—when I was presumed dead?"

"I suppose it is strange."

"Where do you think his soul flew to?"

Marco flushed. "I—I would hope into the loving embrace of his maker."

"I think not."

"Excuse me?"

"I think it flew elsewhere."

"That is an impertinent comment."

"Who is the most impertinent man you ever knew?"

There was a silence.

"It is me, Marco."

The young priest looked at Marco with sparkling eyes.

"It is who?"

"You know very well who."

A chill ran through the Bishop of Padua. The manner of Father Massimo was far different from what he had known it to be—yet it was not unfamiliar. Intellectually he could not comprehend; emotionally he understood perfectly.

"I don't know what you mean," he said in a low voice.

"You do not want to know?"

"I don't know."

"You don't know the man who was once Pope Lando the Second, the Vicar of Christ Upon Earth; the man who was once your cousin, Father Xaverio Torturo?"

"Impossible!—The Pope—My cousin is dead!—Impossible! Impossible!"

"Improbable, yes; impossible, no.—Both before and after the flood, there have been illustrious men who have risen above the laws of the mundane."

"What do you mean?"

"I mean that the one who inhabited this body died and I, I who was the priest Xaverio Torturo, I who was Pope Lando the Second, and later the nameless cripple, transferred my consciousness into his discarded shell."

Marco broke into a sweat. He took a swallow of ginger ale and sat down heavily. The young priest pulled up a chair, the same uncomfortable one that Torturo had always sat in in Vivan's time, and seated himself, crossing one leg over the next.

Father Massimo spoke: "The knowledge of this Art was first imparted to the half brother of Adam by the Holy Spirit. It and other mysteries were engraved on two stone tablets. The story is that after the flood,

Noah, otherwise known as Hermes Trismegistus, found one of these tablets at the foot of Mount Ararat. Since then it has travelled in obscurity through the world; through Egypt, Persia and Chaldaea; through India and Tibet. It has been hinted at in the Kabbalah and in the writings of the Magia; Tibetans such as Marpa the Translator and, more recently I suspect, Christians such as Comte Louis de Chazal and the Abbess of Clermont, Leona Constantia, have been masters (or in the latter case a mistress) of the art. In the *Testamentum novissimum* of Raymond Lulle there are vital hints. To understand the mystery of death has always been the labour of the true philosopher. My sword wore out its sheath; this body you see before you was a fit and useful tool, an opportunity that I could not let slide."

"So . . . So, it is you then, Xaverio?"

"No, it is Father Massimo.—It is Father Massimo, yet with the consciousness of Xaverio Torturo. I have the physical body of the former, whole and handsome, and the latter's soul and thought processes—his memories and will."

"It sounds like a horrible sin!"

"I do not believe it is.—When I transferred my consciousness to this body, the proprietary soul had already flown its cage.—I see you look at me with mingled disbelief and disapproval. As you are one of but few beings who helped me in my time of true need, I will do you the service of uttering a brief explanation.—The manuscript I gleaned this practice from was discovered in an old German Bible in the University library. That such things existed, or were said to exist, I well knew.

268

As I said, in the tradition of the Tibetans, the practice, under the title 'forceful projection' was once common enough. The teacher of Gampopa was the famous Milarepa, whose teacher in turn was Marpa, the translator, who was an expert at it. He received his instruction from Naropa, a remarkable Indian adept, and in turn imparted them to his own son Dharma Dodey. Thus, in the Indian-Tibetan system, the art makes up one of the eight yogas of Naropa, though it was to them unfortunately lost when Dharma Dodey ejected his consciousness into the body of a dead pigeon . . . But it was not lost to the world.—That there has long been a mystical branch of Christianity networking, encompassing the civilised globe is simple fact. That this art was known of by men such as Paracelsus and Albert le Grand, is certain. I laboured over my manuscript and entered into the great meditation, training my consciousness to travel wilfully through the body's spiritual conduits; training, preparing myself for the inevitable eventuality. That I managed to understand the method, to cultivate the art, is provable by my present condition."

Marco looked at the young man, the handsome smiling face and shining eyes across from him. There was something almost comic in the way he who had always been a mild-mannered unboastful individual suddenly had all the mannerisms and bombast of Xaverio Torturo. The bishop did not know whether to be overjoyed or horrified. Was the universe really just a playground where those in the know could go skipping from body to body, one day a Pope the next day a deformity and from that to an athletic figure in its prime?

"God is truly great!" Marco sighed.

Father Massimo smiled. "In the end, he gives each one what they merit," he said.

The sky was mostly blue, though scattered with a few peaceful, cottony clouds. The Tuscan hills, green and cool, smelled of spring: turned earth, the rich aroma of manure, fresh growth and flowers. The hills rolled along, shelved with grapevines sending out their first shoots; dotted with farms and palazzos.

Florence, that great Italian city, the birthplace of men like Michelangelo, Brunelleschi and Machiavelli, geniuses of all time, was in a quiet, cheerful state. The bulk of tourists had not yet come. The weather was fine and, in the afternoon, one could drink a glass of chilled frizzante in the shade.

At Sette Santi, the needy were being fed soup and bread. They sat at large tables set up in the courtyard and chatted to one another cheerfully while the nuns went from man to man, dishing out soup and placing pitchers of water flavoured with lemon and sugar on the table.

At the far end of one table sat a young priest, with a Bible open in front of him from which he read, while slowly chewing bread pills.

The young nun, Sister Justina, approached him.

"Excuse me, Father," she said with a smile, "but this area is for the needy."

He looked up into her hazel eyes. "I am needy," he said.

She blushed. His gaze and voice seemed to be attempting to emphasise a meaning which she did not care to probe.

"I mean," (her voice somewhat agitated). "I mean that this area is for beggars. You must be visiting? Please—come inside and you can eat."

"Let me eat here.—If you don't mind I would rather eat here. It is very pleasant in the sun."

The nun shrugged her shoulders in exasperation. "As you wish," she said and ladled out a portion of soup for the priest.

He ate it joyfully amongst the others—the poverty-stricken, those dressed in rags, their straggling beards hanging in their food and wasted eyes shining with the simple delight of dining. He made conversation with these fellows, each with a life story ready for any ears willing to listen, and then, when the meal was over, began to take the dirty dishes from the table and carry them into the kitchen.

"Oh, please!" Sister Justina said, approaching him. "You don't need to do that. It is my duty."

"It is my pleasure, Sister Justina."

"You know my name?"

"Naturally."

"How so?"

"Because you are the reason I am here," he said, setting the dishes down in the kitchen sink. "I am on a particular mission from Padua to fetch you."

"For what?"

271

"You are to perform daily services in Il Santo, in the Church of Saint Anthony. I am in the process of being made auxiliary bishop. You will be under my jurisdiction."

Just then a sour aroma made him blink and turn. The sensual second chin of the abbess hung palpitating before him and the next moment her upper lip began to tremble.

"What is this?" she said. "I have been waiting in my chamber for the past fifteen minutes for my left thigh to be massaged, and here you are conversing with a man!"

"He is a priest," Sister Justina apologised.

"I am a priest of authority sent from Padua, with papers of notice from your Bishop of Florence."

"Papers of notice?" she sniffed. "What papers of notice?"

"These," he said, removing an envelope from his pocket. "This sister is being removed to our diocese."

"Impossible, she will go nowhere! I need her here to attend to my gout!"

"My dear Mother Barbara," the priest said with a playful smile, "I strongly recommend you apply a little oleum martyr, a little Oil of Lando, to those areas of your person which cause you discomfort. I have not the least doubt in the world that it will cure what ails you. As for Sister Justina, I will call for her and her belongings tomorrow morning—And this," he said, turning to the nun. "And this is for you."

Before either of the two women could say another word, the handsome priest had exited. Sister Justina looked in her hands. They held a blue, woollen cap that she well knew—that which she had woven for a detestable cripple.

The priest, Father Massimo, walked through the streets of Florence, with long, virile strides. His well-polished shoes clicked along the bricks. His face wore an amused expression. He passed the Palazzo Vecchio and the historic fountain by Ammannati. The sun shone on the tops of buildings and onto the Piazza della Signoria. A cloud crawled before it and severed its rays.

www.ingramcontent.com/pod-product-compliance
Lightning Source LLC
Chambersburg PA
CBHW050236110726
47898CB00007B/2178